"I know exactly what I want. I want you to kiss me long and hard."

Madison knew by the glaze of his eyes and his sudden intake of breath that he was going to do it, and it was going to be amazing.

Flint's mouth took hers in a kiss that seared her to her soul. His hands tangled first in her long hair and then slid down her back to her waist. He tugged her closer to him as she opened her mouth to invite him in.

Their tongues danced together in a fiery swirl that half stole her breath away. Her hands rose to his broad shoulders and she gripped them tightly as a deep want rushed through her.

She didn't want just any man...she wanted this man. Her desire for him had nothing to do with her gratefulness. It had nothing to do with his protecting her.

* * *

Be sure to check out the previous books in this exciting miniseries:

Cowboys of Holiday Ranch

Where sun, earth and hard work turn men into rugged cowboys...and irresistible heroes!

* * *

If you're on Twitter, tell us what you think of Harlequin Romantic Suspense! #harlequinromsuspense

Dear Reader,

Having just come home from the Romance Writers of America conference in New York City where I was celebrated for my 150th book with Harlequin, I'm happy that I'm just as excited about this book as I was with the publication of my very first.

Flint McCay is at a crossroads in his life as a cowboy on the Holiday Ranch. He knows the time is quickly approaching when he will have to stop being a cowboy. When that time comes he'll move into the cabin he built in the woods and spend the rest of his life alone.

And then he finds Madison Taylor hiding out in the barn and his life is turned upside down. Madison has secrets, and unless she learns to trust Flint, they are secrets that just might get her killed.

I really hope you enjoy their story and, as always, keep reading!

Carla Cassidy

COWBOY'S VOW TO PROTECT

Carla Cassidy

HARLEQUIN
ROMANTIC
SUSPENSE

HARLEQUIN®
ROMANTIC SUSPENSE™

Recycling programs
for this product may
not exist in your area.

ISBN-13: 978-1-335-62642-4

Cowboy's Vow to Protect

Copyright © 2020 by Carla Bracale

This edition published by arrangement with Harlequin Books S.A.

For questions and comments about the quality of this book,
please contact us at CustomerService@Harlequin.com.

Harlequin Enterprises ULC
22 Adelaide St. West, 40th Floor
Toronto, Ontario M5H 4E3, Canada
www.Harlequin.com

Printed in U.S.A.

Carla Cassidy is an award-winning, *New York Times* bestselling author who has written over 150 novels for Harlequin. In 1995, she won Best Silhouette Romance from *RT Book Reviews* for *Anything for Danny*. In 1998, she won a Career Achievement Award for Best Innovative Series from *RT Book Reviews*. Carla believes the only thing better than curling up with a good book to read is sitting down at the computer with a good story to write.

Books by Carla Cassidy

Harlequin Romantic Suspense

Cowboys of Holiday Ranch

A Real Cowboy
Cowboy of Interest
Cowboy Under Fire
Cowboy at Arms
Operation Cowboy Daddy
Killer Cowboy
Sheltered by the Cowboy
Guardian Cowboy
Cowboy Defender
Cowboy's Vow to Protect

Colton 911

Colton 911: Target in Jeopardy

The Coltons of Red Ridge

The Colton Cowboy

The Coltons of Shadow Creek

Colton's Secret Son

Visit the Author Profile page at Harlequin.com for more titles.

Chapter 1

All of the cowboys from the Holiday Ranch surrounded him. Their fists pummeled him. He tried to defend himself but there were too many of them. Each blow shot pain through him. His ribs screamed in protest and his aching knees finally buckled beneath him. When he fell to the ground they viciously kicked at him. His mouth filled with the coppery taste of blood, even though most of the blows were to his body and not to his face or head.

Help! The plea screamed over and over again in his head, but there was no help coming. In complete defeat, he curled up into a fetal ball on the lush green grass and prayed for it to stop.

Flint McCay came awake suddenly. Pain… it racked his body and for several long moments he didn't move. He stared out the nearby window where the first light of dawn cast slivers of light.

The dream had been so strange. There was absolutely no way the other men on the Holiday Ranch would ever beat him up. They were his brothers. It was a brotherhood forged in painful childhoods and in second chances and them all growing up together here on this ranch.

He winced as he changed positions. No, his pain wasn't from his fellow cowboys. It was from years of his own choices and a recent diagnosis that had unsettled him.

He groaned as he finally moved to a sitting position on the side of the twin-size bed. When Cass Holiday had hired a dozen young runaway boys to work at the ranch, she'd made sure they each had their own rooms in the building the men referred to as the cowboy motel.

Each man had a private room with an adjoining bathroom. The rooms were small, holding only a twin bed and a chest of drawers. It was to the bathroom Flint now headed, hoping a long, hot shower would loosen up tight muscles and ease some of his pain.

Years of bull-riding had taken its toll on him. There wasn't a bone in his body that hadn't been broken or sprained over the years. Now he had a trunk full of trophies, shiny belt buckles and ribbons to show for his success, and a body that at the age of thirty-four felt more like that of a ninety-year-old.

Thankfully, the shower helped and he dressed and headed around the building for the dining room in the back. Most of the cowboys were already there, filling plates from the buffet line Cord Cully, a.k.a. Cookie, prepared for them each and every morning. He also fed the cowboys at lunchtime and dinner.

"Good morning, Flint," Mac McBride greeted him as Flint fell into the line behind him.

"Back at you," Flint replied.

He filled his plate with bacon and scrambled eggs, with biscuits and gravy and added a spoonful of fruit salad. He carried it over to one of the picnic tables where Mac sat with Jerod Steen, Clay Madison and Dusty Crawford.

Flint slid into the seat next to Dusty, who had recently welcomed a baby boy into his life with his wife, Tricia. "How's that kid?" he asked Dusty.

Dusty beamed. "Growing like a weed. How's the cabin coming along?"

Several months ago Flint had bought a couple of acres of heavily wooded land with a clearing perfect for a small house. The cowboys had all pitched in to help him build a cozy, two-bedroom cabin. It was the place he'd live in when he stopped being one of Cassie's cowboys. And whether he liked it or not that time was quickly approaching.

"The furniture was delivered last week and all I have left is to finish putting up a porch and do some trim work," Flint replied.

"It sure is a sweet location with all the trees and that little brook that runs through the backyard," Mac said.

"Yeah, I got lucky in grabbing it before somebody else did," Flint said.

"Do you need some help getting the porch up?" Jerod asked. "You know some of us wouldn't mind coming out to lend you a hand."

"No, thanks. I think I can handle it." The last thing he wanted his friends and fellow cowboys to know about was his weakness…his chronic pain. Besides, he'd accepted enough of their help in getting the place up.

Cowboys didn't complain, and at least for now Flint was still a cowboy. He didn't want to think about what happened when he stopped being a cowboy because the thought scared the hell out of him.

Breakfast continued with talk about the hot months of summer and the lack of rain. They all discussed cattle and chores and whatever else popped into their minds.

"Flint, when are you going to find some nice woman to settle down with?" Dusty asked as they were finishing the meal. "You've got that great cabin, now all you need is somebody to share it with."

"That cabin isn't meant to be shared. Women are just too...too complex for me," Flint replied. "I prefer the company of you all when I'm relaxing in the evenings. Besides, what are you doing picking on me? What about Jerod and Mac? They're both single."

"Hey, don't get me in the middle of this," Mac protested with a laugh.

"Me, neither," Jerod added.

There followed a rowdy debate between the single men and the committed ones, then with breakfast over they all left the dining room to head out for their morning chores.

Thank goodness Flint had it fairly easy this morning. Sawyer Quincy, the newest foreman and one of Flint's "brothers," had delegated him to cleaning up the barn.

The morning was already hot and without a breath of a breeze. August in Bitterroot, Oklahoma, could be brutal. In the barn it would even be hotter. He'd need to remember to hydrate himself throughout the day.

He opened the large barn door and walked in. The barn hadn't been cleaned up since the winter, when hay bales had been pulled out to take to the cattle and horses in the pastures.

Loose hay covered the floor, and bales were helter-skelter around the space. Flint grabbed a rake and began to work on gathering the golden strands into a pile.

As he worked he whistled an old country-western tune that Mac often strummed on his guitar when they gathered in the evenings in the rec room. Those times were when Flint felt the most satisfied, when in the company of men who shared his past, believed in the same core values as he and with whom he had so much in common. And he was going to miss those times when he stopped working on the ranch.

He consciously willed his thoughts away from thinking about his future because the unknown was too daunting to consider. He'd think about that when he absolutely, positively had to. Right now he just wanted to enjoy the smell of the hay and the knowledge that in a few hours he'd share lunch with the men and later that night a few of them would gather in the rec room for more laughs and music provided by Mac and his guitar.

Within an hour he had the hay on the floor swept into neat, small piles that he then bound with twine. He'd just grabbed the hay hook off the wall when he froze. He'd heard…a noise. It hadn't sounded like the faint rustle of a mouse, although there were certainly mice and other small varmints in the barn.

He waited a minute and listened, but heard nothing more so he got back to work. The hay bales weighed about seventy pounds apiece. He began to straighten the stacks, using the hay hook when he needed to lift and carry them from one place to another.

He rounded one corner of the stacks of hay bales and gasped in stunned shock. She was nestled in a little cubbyhole provided by the hay. Her long, dark hair hung in damp ringlets around her heart-shaped face, and her huge blue eyes stared at him both in horror and in fear.

"I'm sorry. I'm so sorry," she said as she hurriedly rose to her feet.

"Maddy, what are you doing here?" he asked in stunned surprise. Maddy Taylor...he knew her from the grocery store where she occasionally checked him out when he shopped there, but he hadn't seen her for the past couple of months. What in the heck was she doing in the middle of the hay in the Holiday barn?

Tears welled up in her eyes. "Please, please don't tell anyone you saw me." Her trembling fingers plucked a strand of the hay out of her long hair. "Don't tell anyone I was here."

"But what's going on?" Shock still fluttered through him at her very presence in the hot barn. How long had she been here and of all places, why was she here? "What are you doing here?"

"I... I was trying to leave town. I have to...to go anyplace but here. My car broke down and...and this was the closest place to walk to…and I just needed some time to figure out what I'm going to do." The words bubbled out of her and her entire body shook like a frightened puppy.

Flint frowned, trying to make sense of what she'd just told him. "When your car broke down why didn't you just try to catch a ride back to your trailer?" He knew she lived in a mobile home park on the wrong side of Bitterroot.

Her eyes widened. "I… I can't ever go back there again."

"Why? Why do you have to leave town?" Bitterroot was a big pond of gossipmongers, but he hadn't heard anything about Maddy in recent days. What in the heck was going on with her?

"Please…don't ask me. I can't tell you. I… I can't tell anyone." Her eyes took on a frightened haunting. "I'm sorry for being here. I'll just get my things and leave." She turned and grabbed the handle of a medium-size, beat-up suitcase that had been half-hidden in the hay.

"Wait…where are you going to go from here?" Flint asked. She had always been thin, but at the moment she looked positively frail. She said she couldn't or wouldn't go back to her trailer. "Where are you going, Maddy? Somebody else's barn? We're having some of the hottest days of the summer right now."

"I… I don't know. I'll figure something out."

Flint took a couple of steps back from her and she walked out of her little hidey-hole with the suitcase in her hand. She was clad in a long blue, sleeveless dress that was wrinkled and damp with perspiration.

"How long have you been in here?" he asked, appalled as he thought of the hot nights and even hotter days.

"Just since last night. My car broke down and I didn't know what to do. I didn't want to stay in the car so this was the closest place to walk to. I'm sorry. I didn't mean to bother anyone. I just need some time to get the car fixed." She started for the barn door.

Flint watched her go, but before she could get all the way to the door he stopped her by calling her name. She turned to look at him. A simmering fear shone from her eyes.

"I have a place you can stay," he said. "It's a cabin in the woods about fifteen miles from here." He couldn't let her…he couldn't let any woman walk out of here with no place to go on such a miserably hot day, especially since he had a place to offer her.

"A…a cabin in the woods?"

He nodded. "Nobody is staying in it right now."

"Who knows about it?"

The question surprised him. "Just a couple of the cowboys here on the ranch. Why?"

"I don't want anyone to find me." Her eyes once again welled up with tears. "I don't want anyone from town to know where I am."

"Nobody will know you're there," he assured her.

"Then, yes, please. I don't want to take advantage of your kindness, but if I could just stay there for a day or two until I can sort out my car issues, I'd really appreciate it."

"Then let's get you out of this hot barn. I'll go and get my truck and I'll pull it up to the door. I'll see you in a couple of minutes."

He left the barn and headed for the vehicle shed in the distance. Thoughts whirled around in his head at a dizzying speed. Why was she hiding out? What had happened to her? It was obvious she was afraid of something or somebody.

Was it possible she had embezzled money from the grocery store and was making her getaway when her car had died? Was she a criminal or a victim of something?

And more important, what was he getting himself involved in by offering her the use of his cabin?

Madison sat in the passenger seat and shot a surreptitious glance to the man who was driving. Around his brown cowboy hat, his shaggy blond hair shone in the sunshine drifting in through the window. He had a strong jawline and a slightly crooked nose and yet that didn't detract from his rugged handsomeness.

Flint McCay. She didn't know much about him, although her heart had certainly fluttered a bit whenever she'd check him out at the grocery store.

He was definitely something of a legend around these parts. He was a champion bull-rider who had successfully ridden some of the biggest and meanest bulls in the rodeos. She also knew he was well liked around town.

She'd never heard anything bad about him, but she knew that didn't mean anything. A man could wear a wonderful facade that drew people to him, but that same man could turn into a horrible monster when there was nobody else around.

Right now she hoped Flint was her savior. She hoped he really was taking her to a cabin in the woods where she could cool off and take a moment to breathe…to think. And she needed to think to figure out how she was going to get out of town as quickly as possible.

"Are you going to tell me what's really going on?" Flint's question broke the silence of the ride.

"There's nothing going on," she lied. "I had just decided to move away from Bitterroot and in the process my car broke down."

He cast her a quick glance, his green eyes filled with skepticism. "If it's as simple as that, then why are you so worried about people knowing where you are?"

"I just don't want anyone trying to change my mind about the move." She knew he didn't believe her. She'd said too much initially when he'd stumbled upon her in the hay and she'd never told so many lies in her life. But the reason she desperately needed to escape Bitterroot was something she'd never speak about aloud. Even if she did, nobody would ever believe her.

As they left the town of Bitterroot behind, a shiver raced through her. She clutched the seat belt fastener with one hand, just in case she had to bail out. Maybe she'd been foolish to trust Flint. Just because he had been pleasant when she'd seen him in the grocery store didn't mean he was really a good guy.

"Relax," he said as if he'd heard her thoughts. "Maddy, I'm not a threat to you. I'm trying to help you."

"And I really, really appreciate it," she replied. It comforted her somewhat that he was a Holiday Ranch cowboy. All the men who had been raised by big Cass Holiday had a reputation for being good, solid men.

Once again they both fell silent. After they had driven a ways, he made a right turn onto a dirt, tree-lined road. They traveled that road for about five minutes and then he made a left turn onto an-

other narrow road where trees encroached on either side. After several more minutes he made a
right turn onto a narrow road that was more of a
trail than a real road.

Trees, casting dark shadows, crowded in and
swallowed up the sunshine. The truck bounced
over ruts in the road and a rabbit ran in front of
them, successfully making it to the other side of
their path.

They were definitely in the middle of nowhere
now. For all she knew they could be in another
state…another country. If he dropped her off by
the side of the road right now she wasn't sure she'd
know how to get back to town.

Tension tightened her shoulders and knotted her
stomach. What was she doing? Was he really taking her to a cabin? Or had she run away from the
devil only to wind up in a different hell?

Then they broke through to a small clearing
where a cabin sat nestled among the trees. It looked
like something out of a fairy tale. A tiny sigh of relief fluttered through her. At least he hadn't lied to
her about there being a cabin.

It was a wooden structure with a big window in
the front. A stone chimney rose up from the roof,
promising warmth on a cold and wintry night. Although the last thing she needed to worry about
right now was winter weather. She just hoped it was
cooler inside the cabin than it had been in the barn.

He pulled up in front and they got out of the truck. He grabbed her suitcase from the back and then together they walked to the front door.

"What is this place?" she asked. Why would Flint have a cabin in the woods when he worked for and lived at the Holiday Ranch?

"It's my future," he said as he opened the door. "Eventually I plan on quitting the Holiday Ranch and when that day comes, I'll move in here." He gestured her inside.

She walked into a small but homey living area. To the right was the refrigerator and stove and cabinets that comprised a small kitchen. A table for two divided the kitchen area from the main living space.

A brown sofa and recliner sat in front of a stone fireplace. To the left of the fireplace a television was mounted on the wall. A bright blue crocheted afghan hung over the back of the sofa, adding a pop of color. There was a cozy warmth to the space with its rich wooden walls and lamps shaped like kerosene lanterns on the end tables.

It was definitely a male space. Other than the afghan, there were no decorative accents suggesting any feminine touches at all, but she admired the natural beauty of the space.

"This is so nice," she finally said as grateful tears welled up in her eyes. "Are you sure it's okay for me to stay here for a day or two?"

He looked away from her and cleared his throat.

"I'm positive. I'll just go and turn on the air-conditioner. It's definitely warm in here." He disappeared through one of the doorways off the main room.

Suddenly, Madison was exhausted. After her car had broken down, she'd walked from her car to the Holiday barn. Then she'd gotten settled in the hay in the barn and had spent most of the night sobbing.

She sank down on the sofa as Flint came back into the room. "The door on the right goes to my bedroom. The door in the middle is the bathroom and the door on the left is a guest room. I'll just put your suitcase in there."

He grabbed the suitcase and once again disappeared. All she wanted now was to sleep, hopefully without dreams. If she just took a nap then surely she'd be able to think more clearly and figure out a real plan for what needed to happen next in her life.

When he returned to the main room, he stuffed his hands in his jeans pockets, jiggled keys and frowned. "Maddy, are you sure there's nothing else you want to tell me?"

"No, but I'd like to ask you for another favor. I hate to ask because you're already doing so much in letting me stay here."

"What is it?"

"I was wondering if you could call the garage and have my car towed in. I don't have a cell phone."

"It wouldn't do you much good out here. The reception is definitely spotty. There's a landline phone on the nightstand next to my bed. But if you want I can make the call to the garage for you."

"Yes, if you don't mind."

He moved toward the front door. "I don't mind." She gave him the specifics of where the car was located and that she'd left the keys under the driver floor mat.

"I should give you my cell phone number in case you think of something else you need. There's a pad and pens in the drawer in the end table."

He pulled out the items and handed them to her. He gave her his cell phone number and she wrote it down. "There are a couple of cold drinks in the fridge, but other than that it's pretty empty. I'll go pick up some supplies for you and bring them back here."

"I can pay you for whatever you spend on me," she replied. She did have some money...all of her life savings was tucked into a bra in her suitcase. Sadly, it wasn't much to start fresh in another town, but she had to make it work. She'd never expected to have to leave Bitterroot behind, but now she had no choice. She had to escape.

"We'll worry about that later. I'll see you in about an hour or so." And with that he went out the door.

She immediately got up and locked the door behind him. She then went to the room where he intended for her to stay. The room was just large enough to hold a queen-size bed and a dresser.

The bed was covered with a white-and-yellow spread, a pleasing complement to the gleaming wooden walls. She stared at her suitcase at the foot of the bed and decided she'd unpack a few things later.

She peeked into his bedroom, where the bed was king-size and covered with an attractive black-and-gray spread. There was also a dresser in this room, but there was nothing on top of it to indicate anyone lived here.

Finally, with her exhaustion tugging heavily on her, she went back into the bedroom where her suitcase sat at the foot of the bed. She tugged it up to the bed and opened it. She wasn't going to completely unpack, but she grabbed clean clothes and then went into the bathroom.

After spending the night in the hay in the hot barn, she desperately needed a shower. She felt dirty and itchy and intended to take advantage of the fact that Flint was gone to take the opportunity of the much-needed shower.

She found a stack of neatly folded towels beneath the sink and a bar of minty fresh-smelling soap already in the shower. There was also a bottle of shampoo on the floor inside the stall.

She took a glorious shower and shampooed her

long hair three times. Then, once clad in a clean summer dress, she beelined for the sofa.

Pulling the blue afghan around her, she marveled that she was in this cabin where for the moment she felt comfortable and safe.

For the moment…

She couldn't know what might happen when Flint returned. Would he expect payment for his kindness? And would he want a different kind of payment other than money? Would he take what he thought she owed him by force?

No…that couldn't happen. She couldn't let that happen. She got up from the sofa and went to the kitchen area. It took her three tries to find the drawer that held a variety of sharp knives. She grabbed the biggest, the meanest-looking one in the drawer and then returned to the sofa.

As she got comfortable once again she squeezed her eyes closed against the heart and soul weariness that had battered her for the past couple of months. She'd never believed there would come a time when she would be so much at the mercy of someone else.

In another lifetime she would have chosen to be with a cowboy like Flint. She'd always assumed that one day she'd marry a cowboy and live happily-ever-after on a ranch. He'd ride the range during the days while she stayed at home and raised babies. She moved her hand to rest on her lower belly.

Those dreams…all her dreams for herself and

for her future had been shattered on a night a little over three months ago. Now the thing that frightened her most was she couldn't see a future for herself. She didn't know where she was going to go or how she was going to survive.

She touched the hilt of the knife, its presence next to her reassuring as she drifted off to sleep.

Chapter 2

Before Flint got out of his car at the grocery store, he made the call to Larry Wright's car dealership and garage to get Maddy's car towed in. Then as he went up and down the grocery store aisles he filled his basket with the kinds of foods he thought a woman would like to eat.

He remembered when he'd taken Jenny Oldham out to dinner she'd ordered a big salad. So he picked up a head of lettuce, a handful of tomatoes and several other fresh vegetables and then added a bottle of ranch dressing to his cart.

He then remembered when he'd taken Laurie Brubaker to the café she'd ordered chicken breast, so he put several packages of that in his cart.

Because he hadn't dated that much it didn't take him long to run out of knowing what else a woman might eat. He picked up staples like milk, bread and eggs and then he just started to pick up random items that he liked and he hoped Maddy liked, as well.

It was a little over an hour later when he headed back to the cabin. As he drove, his thoughts filled with Maddy. He tried to think of all the things he might have heard about her, but there was really nothing to explain her hiding out in the Holiday Ranch barn.

If what she'd told him was the truth, that she had just decided to leave town, then why hadn't she just walked to Cassie's house when her car had broken down? She could have requested a call to the garage and then asked for a ride back to her trailer. Why hide out in a hot, uncomfortable barn?

He didn't get it. But then he didn't get women in general. He found them mysterious alien beings. They were complex and filled with emotions he didn't always understand. He felt awkward in their presence and a couple of years ago he had just given up on dating.

Besides, he'd always envisioned his future alone, especially now. Eventually, when he moved into the cabin and settled in, he might get a dog to keep him company. He was a simple man and all he had to do was figure out what his next job would be.

Cassie paid a fair wage and before her, her aunt Cass had always seen that the men were not only paid well, but also understood the importance of savings and investment.

He'd used up most of his savings on the land and the cabin. He couldn't exactly move to the cabin and retire. Although he'd have no mortgage payment, there would still be utilities and groceries to take care of.

He frowned and gripped the steering wheel more tightly. If not a cowboy, then what would he be? He shoved the troubling question aside as he pulled up in front of the cabin.

Grabbing several of the grocery bags, he then headed for the front door. Finding it locked, he pulled his keys out and unlocked it.

As he walked in he got a quick vision of Maddy asleep on the sofa. Her eyelids fluttered and suddenly she sprang up, her eyes wild with terror as she faced him with a butcher knife in her hand.

She stared at him but he got the impression she wasn't really seeing him. She appeared to still be half-asleep. Her entire body trembled as she raised the knife higher and stepped back from him.

His heart banged against his ribs. "Maddy," he said softly. He didn't move a muscle. She looked like a wild animal and he knew the best way to handle her was to be gentle with her. "It's okay, Maddy. You're safe here." He kept his voice low and smooth. "I promise I'm not going to hurt you. Nobody is going to hurt you here."

Her eyes slowly cleared and she lowered the knife. She appeared to crumble as she fell back to the sofa and began to cry. "I'm sorry. I'm so sorry," she said between tears. "I had a bad dream and then I heard the door open and I… I thought you were a monster."

"There are no monsters here," he replied. "I'm sorry I scared you."

She released a small laugh. "You just walked into your own cabin. I was the crazy lady with the knife. I was way scarier than you were."

He was grateful that her tears had stopped. She got up off the sofa and sat at the table. He set the grocery bags on the counter and then turned to her. "There's a couple more bags in the truck. I'll be right back."

Whew. He stepped outside and drew several deep breaths. His heart had definitely accelerated when she'd faced him with that knife. What in the hell had happened to her to warrant her taking a nap with a weapon? And then raise it to him as if she was terrified for her personal safety.

He'd known if necessary he would have been able to take the knife away from her. He was just grateful it hadn't gotten to that point. He grabbed the last two grocery bags out of the back of his truck and then returned to the cabin.

"I apologize again," she said. "Nothing like greeting a man in his own home with a knife."

"Don't worry about it. It's already forgotten." He opened a bag of the groceries and began to pull out the contents. "I wasn't sure what you liked so I tried to get a little bit of everything."

"How much do I owe you?"

"We'll worry about all that later." He opened the fridge door and began to put the vegetables inside.

It was obvious she had showered and changed her dress. She now wore a loose-fitting pink sundress that complemented her dark hair and blue eyes.

She not only smelled of minty-fresh soap, but also of a field of sweet wildflowers. A whisper of desire blew through him. It was as unexpected as it was inappropriate. He'd always found Maddy very pretty but that was the last thing he needed to be thinking about her right now.

"I can at least help you put the groceries away." She got up from the table and opened another bag.

It took them only a few minutes to put the groceries away and then once again she sat at the table and he stood with his back against the fridge.

"There's a couple of things I wanted to tell you," he said. "First of all, help yourself to anything you want and let me know if there's something else you need that isn't here."

"I can't imagine needing anything more than what you've already provided."

He shoved his hands in his pockets. "I'd also like to ask you if it's okay that while you're here I can continue work here. I want to get a porch up and there's more trim work to finish. Normally, I'm out here around five-thirty and I work until about eight in the evenings and then I go back to the ranch. Is that going to be a problem for you?"

"Of course not," she replied after only a moment's hesitation. "I wouldn't want to be responsible for you not getting your work done here."

"Did somebody hurt you, Maddy?"

He could tell the question took her by surprise. She held his gaze for a long moment and then looked away. "Flint, I really appreciate what you're doing for me, but please don't ask me any questions."

She definitely had secrets…seemingly dark secrets, but she was here for only a short period of time and it was really none of his business.

"All right, then," he replied and straightened. "I need to get back to the ranch. I'll see you again this evening."

"I'll see you then." She followed him to the door and the last thing he heard was her locking it after him.

He was almost grateful she hadn't told him what was going on. He didn't want to know too much about her, especially given that unexpected touch of desire that had momentarily swept through him.

Still, he couldn't help but be curious. It was damned strange for a woman to take a knife to bed with her when she was sleeping. And he couldn't erase from his mind that look of sheer terror that had been in her eyes when she'd jumped up from the sofa.

When he got back to the ranch he pulled into the shed and then headed toward the barn to finish the cleanup. "Hey, Flint." The deep voice came from behind him.

He turned to see Mac hurrying toward him. "Everything all right?" Mac asked, a frown of worry across his forehead.

"Yeah, everything is fine. Why?"

"I came to help you in the barn, but you weren't there. Then when I saw your truck was missing I just got a little concerned that something might have happened to you."

"Sorry to worry you," Flint replied. "I had some personal errands to run. I should have told somebody I was leaving." Of course, there had been no way to tell anyone what was happening because he'd promised Maddy he wouldn't. And Flint wouldn't break that promise.

"As long as everything is okay, that's all I care about." Mac clapped him on the back. "Ready to knock out the rest of the barn?"

"Ready," Flint replied.

Together the two of them went back inside where they stacked hay and talked about the hot weather, the work at the ranch and the health of the cattle and horses.

The topic then turned to Mac's music. "I don't understand why you never wanted more than just entertaining a bunch of cowboys after a long day at work," Flint said. "Hell, you sound better than most of the singers I hear on the radio."

"Oh, there was definitely a time I thought I'd sing in front of huge audiences and tour the country in a big RV. I'd be wealthy, and adoring female fans would throw their underwear on the stage."

Flint laughed. "All of that sounds pretty good except the underwear part." He sobered. "So what happened?"

"I grew up and I found my home here. The only audience I really want now is a special woman and eventually a couple of kids."

"Speaking of women, have you ever heard any gossip about Maddy Taylor dating anyone?"

Mac looked at him in surprise. "Maddy from the grocery store?"

Flint nodded, wondering why the heck he had even asked.

"I've never heard any gossip of any kind about her. And, I've definitely never heard anything about who she might be dating. Why?" Mac looked at him in amused speculation.

"I was just curious. I haven't seen her at the grocery store for a while and I wondered what might have happened to her."

"Now that you mentioned it I haven't seen her around lately, either," Mac replied. "So what's your interest?" His amusement was back sparkling in his eyes. "She's a mighty pretty young woman."

Flint forced a laugh. "I've got no interest in her like that. I was just in the grocery store earlier and she popped into my mind and I realized I hadn't seen her there for a while." He really wished he hadn't brought it up at all.

Thankfully, the conversation turned to other topics. By four-thirty the barn was all cleaned up and the two men headed to their rooms to shower before dinner.

As Flint showered, he couldn't help that his thoughts remained on the woman in his cabin. Something had happened to her, something bad. She'd always been a bright ray of sunshine in the grocery store, but the sunshine was nowhere inside the Maddy who had jumped off his sofa and wielded a knife. What had happened to her?

None of your business, cowboy, a little voice whispered over and over again in his head. She'd told him not to ask questions and he would abide by her wishes. Besides, her car had been towed and as soon as it was fixed she'd be out of his cabin and off to wherever she intended to go.

He ate dinner with the other men and then left to head back to the cabin. He knew his time on the Holiday Ranch was drawing to the end. His aching body was like a ticking time bomb and he wanted the cabin to be completely finished when the bomb eventually went off.

He was eager to get started on the porch. The concrete had already been poured and the posts were set. All the wood he needed had been delivered a week ago. So now all he had to do was lay the floor and build a roof.

There were deer and all kinds of other wildlife in these woods and he could easily envision himself in the future sitting on the porch in the early mornings when the deer came out to wander and birds sang their musical songs.

Even though he had only spent a couple of nights there, when he pulled up in front of the cabin there was a sense of homecoming for him.

To his surprise Maddy opened the front door, apparently having heard his truck pull up. "Hey," she said as he got out of the truck.

She looked considerably better than she had earlier in the day. Her eyes were as clear as the blue Oklahoma sky and the smile she offered him appeared slightly tentative, but genuine.

"I'm just going to work out here for a while," he

said as he pulled a toolbox out of the pickup bed and set it on the ground.

"No problem," she replied. "I noticed you have one of those fancy pod coffeemakers inside and lots of pods, but I don't drink coffee. Would you like me to make you a cup and bring it out here to you?"

Once again he looked at her in surprise. He wasn't accustomed to any woman doing anything for him. "Sure, that sounds great."

"How do you drink it?"

"Just black is fine."

She went back inside and he grabbed several planks of the pine deck wood from the pile on the side of the house and moved it closer to where it would be used.

He tried not to think about how odd it was that Maddy Taylor was inside his cabin and making him a cup of coffee. Everything felt so surreal since the moment he'd found her hiding in the hay in the barn.

She came out carrying the cup of coffee. "Thanks," he said as he took the cup from her. "Have you eaten?"

"Yes, thank you. I made myself some scrambled eggs and toast a little bit earlier," she replied. She looked at the wood. "So you're going to make a front porch?"

"A covered porch." Flint took a sip of the brew. "Eventually, I plan to sit on the porch and see the deer that frequent this area while I drink my morning coffee."

"Oh, that sounds like that would be wonderful. Do you mind if I sit out here and watch you work for a little while? It's so pleasant out here with the tree shade."

"Uh…sure. I've got a lawn chair you can use." He went to the side of the house where a fold-up lawn chair leaned against the cabin. He grabbed it, carried it around and opened it so she could sit just out of the way of his work.

He wasn't sure why she wanted to sit out here. He'd never had an audience when he worked before and he found the whole thing rather awkward.

Since everything was ready for him to lay the deck, he began by placing the long pine planks down. By this time of night his back and hip joints were usually screaming in pain and tonight was no different.

He swallowed the groans that threatened to escape from him each time he bent over. He was acutely aware of her and there was no way in hell he'd want her or anyone else to see or hear his pain.

"It's so beautiful here," she said.

"Yeah, it is," he agreed. He grabbed the hammer and a handful of nails from his toolbox.

"How did you ever find this place?"

"Dan Griffin at the realty office found it for me.

The minute I saw it, I knew it was the right place for me."

"So are you thinking of moving here soon?" A light breeze lifted several strands of her hair and the waning sunlight caressed her delicate features.

Oh, she was definitely a distraction. Flint had never really noticed just how pretty she was until now. Her eyes were lined with long, dark lashes and her lips were puffy pillows that invited a kiss.

Jeez, what was wrong with him? Why was he even thinking these thoughts? He wasn't about to kiss her. He didn't want a woman in his life. Besides, he didn't even know her and in any case she was only here until her car got fixed.

She'd asked him a question but damned if he could remember what it was right now. "Uh, I need to hammer down these planks," he said.

"Oh, I'm sorry. I don't want to keep you from your work." Her eyes suddenly widened and she jumped up from the chair. She raced toward the trees and then bent over and threw up.

Madison's stomach rolled with nausea. After throwing up once, she raced into the house, vaguely aware of Flint running after her in alarm. She ran into the bathroom and threw up once again, at the same time waving Flint away. "I'm okay," she finally managed to say to him.

The nausea had finally passed. She closed the

bathroom door and rinsed her mouth several times and then brushed her teeth. Thank goodness she'd set her toothbrush in the bathroom earlier. Oh God, how embarrassing. The last thing a woman ever wanted a man…any man…to see was her tossing her cookies.

She opened the bathroom door to find Flint on the other side, his handsome features wreathed with worry lines. "Maddy, are you okay?"

"I'm fine," she assured him. "I just got a sudden bout of nausea. It's all gone now."

"Was it maybe the eggs? You told me you made scrambled eggs earlier. I didn't check the date on them. Things are usually pretty fresh at the grocery store."

"No, I'm sure it wasn't the eggs. I… I've just always had a ridiculously weak stomach." At the moment she was just tired. "Really, Flint, I'm okay."

The concern remained on his face. "If you say so."

She stepped out of the bathroom. "I think maybe I'll just stretch out on the sofa for a little while. I didn't get any sleep last night and that might have contributed to my upset stomach."

"Okay. I'll be right outside if you need me for anything."

Minutes later he was back outside and she was on the sofa. She was disappointed. She had been hoping for a little more conversation with Flint.

She didn't care what they talked about; she'd just wanted a little nonthreatening human interaction.

For almost three months she'd been locked up in her trailer, not speaking to or interacting with anyone. She'd quit her job and had her groceries and anything else she'd needed delivered to her house. The only place she'd ventured out during that time was to the library a couple of times.

It had been fear and trauma that had locked her inside the trailer. The utter loneliness had come soon after. Normally, she was a social animal. She'd loved working at the grocery store where she got to visit with people as they came through her line to check out.

It was amazing how much people would tell her about themselves, about their lives, when she was scanning their food items. It was also pretty amazing how much you could learn about people just by seeing what food they chose to put in their home.

Bang. Bang. Bang. The sound of Flint's hammer hitting wood sounded. She closed her eyes. These nausea bouts never lasted long but always left her tired. Hopefully, in fifteen or twenty minutes or so, she'd feel like going back outside to watch Flint.

And in the brief moments she'd been outside, watching him had been a pleasure. In his dark brown T-shirt and jeans, he was a long, lean glass of hunk.

Despite his leanness, his arms were firmly muscled and his shoulders were broad. He was the type of man she might have once dreamed about. She didn't dream anymore. She only had nightmares. And she always dreaded the coming of night.

At least for tonight she'd have a real bed rather than the hay in a barn like she'd had last night. She couldn't believe the good luck that it had been Flint who had found her and he'd had a place to bring her, a place that, according to him, few people knew about.

The car repairs shouldn't cost too much and could be finished quickly so she could be on her way as far away from Bitterroot, Oklahoma, as possible. It was the only way she would be safe.

As the dark shadows of twilight began to fall, she got up and turned on the lamps on either end table. They provided a cozy, warm golden glow, but they couldn't stop the anxiety that bubbled up inside her as night approached.

You're safe here, an inner voice whispered in her head. *Nobody can hurt you here.* Except Flint. She frowned. So far Flint had been nothing but courteous and respectful toward her. Rationally, she knew not all men were monsters and so far there wasn't a hint of monster in Flint.

The hammering halted and moments later a soft knock fell on the door. He opened the door and peeked his head in. "I just wanted to check to see if you were all right before I head out of here for the night."

She motioned him inside and got up off the sofa. "Would you like another cup of coffee before you head back to the ranch?" She just wanted him to stay for a bit and talk to her, to ward off the terror of the night by ending the evening with a little conversation.

He looked at her in surprise. "Uh...okay."

"Please, sit and let me make it for you." She hurried over to the coffee machine and placed a pod in it as he washed his hands in the sink. He then moved to the table and sat.

"Did you get a lot of work done?" she asked.

"I got about half of the deck laid. Be careful if you go outside. I wouldn't want you to trip and hurt yourself."

"I have no intentions of venturing outside of this cabin until my car is ready or you're here," she replied. She carried the coffee to him and then sat across the table from him.

"Oh, that reminds me. I told Larry at the car dealership to call the number here in the cabin so he can speak with you directly about whatever repairs are needed."

"Thank you," she replied. "Hopefully, I'll hear from him soon."

He curled his hands around the coffee cup. His hands were large and work-worn and she wondered...darn, what was wrong with her? Why would she even wonder what those hands might feel like stroking up and down her back? That was the last thing she should be thinking about.

"So do you have a particular destination in mind when you leave here?" he asked.

"I'm thinking maybe someplace in Wyoming."

"Have you ever been there before?"

"No, but I've read a lot of books set there." Romance books. She'd read a lot of romance books set in Wyoming where the winters were cold and the cowboys were hot. Of course no cowboy would ever want her now. Nobody would want her.

"I've heard it's beautiful country," he replied.

An awkward silence ensued and his gaze seemed to go everywhere in the room but on her. "So once you finish the porch is the cabin all done?" she finally asked.

His dark green eyes found hers once again. "For the most part. I still need to trim out my bedroom and take care of a few odds and ends, but nothing major. I don't know if you noticed it or not but there's a detached garage in the back and that still needs a bit of work."

"I didn't notice. I have to confess, I spent most of the day sleeping."

"Nothing wrong with that, especially if you've picked up a bit of a flu bug."

Her face warmed. "I'm sure I'm fine," she assured him. "I'm sorry about throwing up in your trees."

He smiled at her. It was the first real smile she'd seen since he'd found her hiding in the barn. The gesture crinkled the corners of his eyes and exuded warmth that instantly washed over her.

"Maddy, I spend my time with a bunch of cowboys who sometimes get rowdy on a Saturday night. They drink too much and upchuck in all kinds of places. I'm sure my trees will be just fine."

"I'm just glad you aren't mad."

He raised a blond eyebrow. "Why would I get mad at you about getting sick?"

"I don't know…so, what does make you mad?" she asked tentatively. It suddenly seemed vitally important that she know this about him, especially if they were going to spend a little time together.

He frowned, obviously in thought. "The usual things that make most people mad: injustice and abuse, especially abuse of women and children. I also don't much like people who abuse animals. But other than those things, I'm a pretty laid-back guy. There isn't much that anyone does in my personal life to upset me." He finished his coffee. "And on that note, I need to head back to the ranch."

Even though she still wasn't sure she could trust him, she almost hated to see him go. So far his presence made her feel safe rather than threatened in any way.

"Then I guess I'll see you about the same time tomorrow night?" She walked with him to the front door. "By then I should have news about my car."

"Whatever. Maddy, if you need to stay a day or two longer, don't worry about it. And if you need anything don't hesitate to call me."

And then he was gone and she was alone in the night. She sat on the sofa and thought about turning on the television, but she instantly rejected the idea. She wanted to hear if any threat…if any danger came close and she wouldn't be able to hear that if the television was playing.

Even though Flint had said that only a few of the cowboys on the Holiday Ranch knew of this place, she couldn't be absolutely sure of that.

The people in Bitterroot loved to gossip and it was totally possible one of those men had mentioned this place while drinking at the Watering Hole, or having dinner at the café. And then that person mentioned it to somebody else who mentioned it to somebody else and so on…

"Stop it," she whispered aloud to herself. Her brain was overworking in an effort to freak her out, and she couldn't allow that to happen. She had to stay calm.

Still, she decided to turn off the living area lights and go into her bedroom. With the lights off in the front of the cabin, anyone driving up would think nobody was here. Even though she hoped she wouldn't have to use it, she carried the butcher knife into her bedroom and placed it beneath the pillow.

Once there she changed out of her dress and into a nightshirt. The lamp next to the bed emitted a soft glow and thankfully, when she'd left the trailer she'd thrown a few paperback books into her suitcase.

The bed seemed to envelop her in softness and she snuggled in and opened one of the books. But there was no escaping reality tonight.

Even though she held the book in her hand, her thoughts were far away from the words printed on the page. She'd told Flint she'd like to go to Wyoming and maybe she would. But she would mourn leaving Bitterroot, which had been her home for the past twenty-eight years.

Her childhood had certainly been difficult, but over the past ten years she'd made a cozy home for herself in the trailer. It had been her happy sanctuary until…

She squeezed her eyes tightly closed and drew in several deep, steadying breaths. She couldn't go there. If she allowed her mind to take her back, she would be in the throes of a post-traumatic stress episode.

"Just breathe," she whispered to herself. She closed her eyes and drew in deep breaths. What she needed to do was pray the car repairs didn't cost too much or take too long so she could leave here for anywhere else. She must have fallen asleep for the next time she opened her eyes, early-morning sunshine was drifting through the window. She'd made it through the night without any nightmares or disturbances.

She showered and dressed for the day and then opened the door in the kitchen that led outside. There was a small porch and in the short distance was the garage.

The clean, fresh-scented air tickled her nose as birds sang their early-morning songs. Despite her circumstances a wave of optimism swept through her.

She hoped to hear from Larry Wright at the car dealership today. And she hoped the repairs were minimal and she could be on her way. Tomorrow was Sunday so if she didn't hear about her car today then it would be Monday before she heard anything.

She didn't want to be here any longer than necessary. The longer she stayed the more possibility that somebody would find her here.

Besides, if she stayed too long here in this cozy cabin she knew she would never want to leave. Right now she felt so safe here, but she had to go.

This wasn't her place. She didn't know where her place was right now, but it wasn't here. It couldn't be anywhere near Bitterroot.

While she ate breakfast she found herself wondering why Flint was leaving the Holiday Ranch. Did he intend to work on the ranch and live here? Or did he plan to quit working there? And if he was quitting the ranch, then what did he intend to do? Maybe buy some land where he could be his own boss on a ranch?

She couldn't remember specifically what he had told her, not that it was any of her business. All she had to worry about was getting her car fixed and then picking a place to start over in a new life.

Wherever she ended up landing, she had to hit the ground running. It was imperative that she find a place to live and a job as soon as possible. The rent on her trailer was paid up through the next two months. She was hoping that within that time she'd get an opportunity to rent a truck and move her furniture and other items to her new place.

She read a little and then by around two o'clock she wandered the cabin restlessly. Since it was Saturday she wondered if Flint might come earlier than he had yesterday.

She hoped so. She liked talking to him. She also liked looking at his handsome, tanned and slightly weathered face. He carried with him the scent of the outdoors, of sunshine and wind along with a hint of a fresh-scented cologne.

Part of the reason she liked talking to him was that when she was engaged in conversation she had no time to think about what had happened or how messed up her life had become.

The silence pressed in around her as the minutes and then hours ticked by. She made herself dinner and then at a few minutes after five, she heard the sound of an approaching vehicle. She looked out the window to make sure it was him, and then she flung open the door and stepped out onto the half-finished porch deck.

"Hi, cowboy," she said when he got out of his truck.

A slow grin curved his lips. "Well, hello to you."

"Did you have a good day?" she asked as he pulled his red toolbox out of the bed of his pickup.

"I had a fine day. What about you?" He bent over and set the toolbox next to where he would be working to lay the rest of the deck. When he straightened to look at her, she thought she heard a soft groan escape his lips. He cleared his throat and his smile widened. "You look well rested."

"Having a bed to sleep in is way better than a hay-covered floor in a hot barn. Would you like me to make you a cup of coffee?"

"That sounds good, but you know you don't have to wait on me, Maddy."

"It's just a cup of coffee, Flint, not a five-course meal," she teased.

"I wouldn't like a five-course meal…it takes too long to get to the meat and potatoes."

She laughed. "I'll be right back with the coffee."

When she returned outside with the hot drink she was pleased to see that he had set up the lawn chair for her. He took the cup from her and her heart fluttered just a little bit when their fingers touched. Jeez, what was wrong with her?

She sat in the chair and watched him take a sip of the coffee. "I was hoping to hear something about my car today, but I didn't."

"When I spoke to Larry he told me he had a few cars ahead of yours. I'm sure they'll get to it sometime on Monday." He took another drink of the coffee and then set the cup down in the grass.

"I don't want to take advantage of your kindness for too long," she replied.

Once again that slow smile curved his lips. "Does it look like you're bothering me?"

"No." Why did his smile shoot a burst of warmth through her? She had assumed after what had happened to her she'd never feel that kind of way about a man again. "Still, as soon as my car is ready I promise I'll be out of your hair."

"Whenever." He carried several boards next to the deck and began to lay them in place. "Is Maddy your given name?" he asked.

"My given name is Madison," she replied.

"Madison. That's pretty. Why don't you use it instead of Maddy?"

Madison…she liked the way her name sounded

falling from his lips. Nobody ever called her that, but she'd always thought of herself as Madison. "I don't know. My father always called me Maddy and so that's how everyone knew me."

"If you don't mind then I'd like to call you Madison."

She smiled and another sweet warmth blossomed inside her. "I would like that."

She watched as he began to hammer down the boards. She hadn't been outside more than ten minutes when the nausea began. Oh no, not again. She tried to ignore it. Then she tried to breathe through it, but neither of those techniques helped.

She jumped up and ran into the house and made it to the bathroom just in time to throw up. She threw up two more times and then the nausea slowly passed. She waited a couple of minutes to see if it would return, but it didn't. Once again she rinsed her mouth and then brushed her teeth.

When she opened the bathroom door Flint stood on the other side. Concern darkened his eyes and a grim determination tightened his features.

"Madison, you need to see a doctor," he said. "It's obvious something is wrong with you."

"I'm fine," she replied. She pushed past him and into the living room area.

"You aren't fine," he replied firmly. "You're sick and you need to see a doctor," he repeated.

"Really, it's okay, Flint. I'm okay." She definitely didn't want to be having this conversation.

"If you don't want to see a doctor in town then maybe I can get Dr. Washington to come out here to see you."

"Please, just leave it alone, Flint." Desperation filled her. She turned and started to walk away from him.

"I can't leave it alone," he replied. "Madison, you've thrown up two evenings in a row. Something is obviously wrong and right now you're under my care."

She whirled around to face him once again. "I'm not sick… I'm… I'm pregnant." The minute the words left her lips she crumbled onto the sofa and began to cry.

Chapter 3

"Pregnant?" Flint stared at her in stunned surprise. That was the last thing he expected to hear. "Don't cry," he told her, hating the tears that slid down her cheeks as tiny sobs escaped her.

"Madison, please don't cry." Hell, he didn't know what to do with a crying woman…a pregnant crying woman at that.

"I… I…can't help it. I di…didn't want anyone to know," she replied.

He shoved his hands in his pockets and jostled with his keys as he approached the sofa. "What can I do to make you stop crying? If I sing for you, will you stop? I'll warn you I have a terrible singing voice. Mac always says when I was born the

doctors should have twisted my vocal chords together to see if they could get anything better than
croaks like a frog."

A small laugh escaped her. It was exactly what
he'd hoped to accomplish. He sank down next to
her on the sofa as she stopped sobbing and instead
began to wipe the tears off her cheeks.

"I won't tell anyone, Madison. Your secret is
safe with me. I swear I won't tell anybody." He
hesitated a moment and then continued, "So who
is the father? Can't he help you out with whatever
is going on?"

She dropped her hands to her lap. "There is no
father." She didn't meet his gaze.

"Madison, there has to be a father," Flint said
gently.

"Not in this case." Her gaze returned to his and
her chin lifted with a hint of defiance.

"So it was one of those immaculate concep-
tions," he replied. "I have to say, it's been a while
since one of those happened."

Her cheeks flushed with a hot-pink color. "Okay,
so there was a sperm donor, but he will never be
a part of my life and he definitely will never be in
this baby's life." Tears once again filled her eyes.

"Is this why you want to leave town?"

"It's one of the reasons, but I have other reasons, too."

He could tell by the look in her eyes that she

wasn't going to share any of those with him. "Madison, don't you need to see a doctor? You're getting sick every evening."

"It's morning sickness, Flint, only I have it in the evenings. It should be passing soon."

He eyed her with concern. "I thought morning sickness only happened in the mornings." Her wild-flower scent threatened to distract him, but the conversation was far too important for any distraction.

"Morning sickness can happen anytime in the day."

"Did a doctor tell you that?"

Her cheeks grew pink once again and her gaze skittered away from his. "I haven't seen a doctor."

"Then how do you know what you're talking about?" He didn't want to pry. He just wanted to make sure she was really okay.

"I went to the library and researched everything I could find on the subject." Her gaze sought his again. "I'm fine, Flint. I promise you, there's nothing for you to worry about. Besides, it's not your job to worry about me."

"Shouldn't you see a doctor?" he asked again. She could tell him to not worry about her, but he couldn't help it.

"Not in this town. I'll see one as soon as I get settled wherever I'm going. Now, I'm sure you're eager to get back to your work on the porch before the sun goes down."

It was a dismissal. Reluctantly, he rose. "You'll let me know if you need something special from the grocery store or the drugstore?"

She smiled at him. It was one of those sunshine smiles he remembered seeing on her face months ago. "You're a very nice man, Flint McCay."

A touch of warmth filled his face. "Thanks. I'll just be outside if you need anything."

Pregnant.

He walked around the cabin to the garage to retrieve his ladder, and his brain tried to work through the shock her secret had given him.

She must have been dating somebody to get in the condition she was in. Maybe when she told the man she was dating that she was pregnant, he'd reacted badly. No, that didn't seem right because she didn't want anyone to know about the pregnancy and that implied she hadn't told the father-to-be.

As he began work on the porch roof, his mind continued to go through different scenarios. Maybe she and her lover just had a big fight and Madison decided on a whim to pack up and leave. Was that really what this was all about? A lover's spat that had spun out of control? But even that didn't feel right, not when he remembered the terror in her eyes.

Still, Flint believed the father had a right to know about the baby. He would never want a woman he dated to get pregnant and not tell him about the baby. Fathers had rights, too. He frowned. But if the man was abusive then all bets were off.

Maybe by the time her car was fixed she'd change her mind about leaving town. She'd reconcile with her boyfriend and they'd raise their baby together.

Flint had never known his own father. His mother hadn't even known who his father was. He'd always wondered how his horrible childhood would have been better if his father had been in his life.

He reminded himself that Madison and her choices weren't any of his business. Still, he hated to think of her pregnant and all alone in a strange, new place. Maybe he could talk her into going back to her trailer and staying here in Bitterroot. Surely she had friends in town who would help her. Heck, she could consider him a new friend who would do whatever he could to help her out.

He worked until the sun gave its last gasp and then he put his tools and ladder away and walked to the front door. He knocked and she answered.

"Coffee?" she asked. Her eyes seemed to simmer with a kind of faint desperation.

"Sure," he replied. Like the night before he washed up in the sink and took a seat at the table while she made his cup of coffee.

"Are you feeling better now?" he asked as she put the coffee before him and then sat across from him.

"Much better. The nausea only lasts a few minutes and once it's gone, it's gone for the rest of the night."

He took a sip of the hot drink and tried not to notice how pretty she looked. She wore a blue T-shirt that made her eyes appear even bluer. A pair of jeans hugged her still-slender body.

She was definitely easy on the eyes, not that it mattered to him. It also didn't matter that whenever he was near her his body subtly warmed. He wasn't looking for a woman in his life, but her current situation definitely concerned him. He wanted to somehow help her, but he wasn't sure how, especially if she wasn't going to share with him what was really going on.

At the moment he felt the same awkwardness he always felt when in the company of an attractive woman. He took another sip of his coffee and then stared down at the cup, trying to think of some way to get a little more information from her concerning the baby's father.

"So tell me something about yourself, Flint," she asked. "I know you were one of Cass Holiday's lost boys, but tell me how you got lost."

Everyone in town knew the story of the "lost boys" at Cass's ranch. When Cass Holiday's husband had died all her ranch help had walked out on her, believing she wasn't strong enough, wasn't smart enough, to run the big spread.

With the help of a social worker in Oklahoma

City, Cass had staffed her ranch with young run-away boys who, for one reason or another, had vowed they would or could never go home again. Flint had been one of those boys.

"Or maybe you don't want to talk about that," she added hurriedly. "I don't want to pry."

"No, I don't mind." Maybe if he shared a little bit about his past life, it would help her trust him enough to tell him more about hers.

He drew a deep breath and once again looked down in his coffee cup as he accessed old, bad memories. He rarely thought of his childhood. He'd always considered that his life had really begun on the day he'd arrived at the Holiday Ranch.

"I don't remember a time when my mother wasn't a drug addict. What I do remember is back-alley dope deals, scary men in and out of our lives, and always moving from one dump to the next."

He was deep in his memories now. "Initially she must have been doing meth. She'd be up for days and flying high. One time when I told her I was hungry, she swooped me up and danced me around the room and told me we didn't need to eat. We could just live on peace and happiness. Of course little boys just sometimes need real food."

"Oh, Flint, I'm so sorry." He looked up into her warm, sympathetic gaze. "Was that what made you decide to run away?"

"No, it wasn't that. I was too young then to even

think about running away. It was when she ex-
changed meth for heroin that things took a really
bad turn."

He looked past her shoulder and continued, "I'd
find her nodded out on the bathroom floor, or in her
car with a needle still stuck in her arm. I begged
her to stop. I begged her to get help, but she told me
she loved the stuff and she was never going to stop.
I tried to take care of her when she was dope sick.
I'd clean up her vomit and I'd wipe her down when
she was sweating and coming out of her own skin.
I prayed every day that she wouldn't die."

He'd suppressed these memories for so long and
now they unfurled in his brain like distant nightmares. As a child he'd been half-starved and rarely
clean. His mother had used him to gain people's
sympathy and cash when they panhandled. He'd
never, ever felt loved by her.

He looked back at Madison. "I loved my mother,
but I learned pretty early on that she couldn't love
me back. But I knew I was watching her die. Finally, when I was thirteen I realized I couldn't do
anything to help her and I wasn't going to stay
around there and watch her die, so I left."

It was the most words he had used at any one
time and he was surprised by the emotion that filled
his chest. Grief battled with guilt, a guilt that he
had chosen to save himself instead of sticking by
his mother's side.

Carla Cassidy 61

But there had been days and days of homelessness. When they did have a roof over their heads, it was usually a drug house where other addicts came to use. He'd seen his mother beaten and abused, and the taste of fear never left his mouth.

Madison's touch to the back of his hand brought him back from that frightening place. "Sorry, that was probably way more information than you wanted," he said ruefully. In fact, he'd just told her things that he'd never shared with anyone else.

"I'm just sorry you had to go through that." She drew her hand back from his and instantly he felt a strange bereavement. He'd liked her touch. For just a brief moment he'd felt an odd connection to her.

"So what's your story?" he asked.

She changed positions on the chair. "While my childhood wasn't as horrifying as yours, we share a lot in common. My mother died from breast cancer when I was eight and my father was a raging alcoholic. What he wanted when my mother was gone, was to leave Bitterroot and start a single life someplace else, but unfortunately I was the albatross around his neck and he never, ever let me forget that he was stuck in Bitterroot because of me."

Her pretty eyes darkened. "When I was young, he at least tried to hide his drinking, but by the time I was about twelve he didn't even attempt to hide it. I'd find him passed out all over the house and I'd clean him up and get him into bed. The worst times were when he'd go out in the evenings to go to the Watering Hole. I'd wake up every morning hoping and praying that he'd made it home and wasn't dead in a ditch. I don't know why I cared. He never said a nice thing to me. I never felt his love, only his disdain and resentment toward me."

He was surprised by his desire to touch her, to somehow take the darkness of her childhood out of her eyes, out of her memories. Before he could do anything like that, she released a laugh.

"And that was probably way more information than you wanted," she said.

"Not at all," he assured her. "I'm just sorry you had to live with that. So is your father still around?"

She shook her head. "Heavens, no. On the morning of my eighteenth birthday he packed up his truck with his personal belongings, told me I was on my own and he drove off and I never saw or heard from him again."

He knew instinctively that now wasn't the time to press her on any details about her pregnancy or try to change her mind about her choice to leave town.

"So you've been on your own since then?" he asked.

She nodded. "I got the job at the grocery store and paid my way. I've eaten a lot of Ramen noodles through the years when money got really tight, but I survived my father leaving me all on my own."

"That took a lot of strength at that young age," he said.

"I imagine it took you a lot of strength to run away when you're thirteen years old," she replied.

She gazed at him for a long moment. And it was finally he who looked away. The fact that he wouldn't mind sitting here and talking to her longer unsettled him. Besides, it was getting late. "This has been nice, but I need to head out." He drained the last of his coffee and carried the cup to the sink. She got up from the table and walked with him to the door.

"Thanks, Flint."

He looked at her in surprise. "For what?"

"For coming in and spending some time with me. I like talking with you."

"I like talking to you, too," he replied. He was surprised to realize it was the truth. She was fairly easy to talk to. In fact, it still vaguely surprised him that he'd spoken so much about his past with his mother to her.

They said their good-nights and Flint got into his truck and headed back to the ranch. She liked talking to him. No woman had ever said that to him before and her words shot an unexpected warmth through him.

Suddenly, he couldn't wait until the next night when he'd get an opportunity to talk with her again.

* * *

Monday just after noon Flint headed into town to pick up some supplies for Cookie and a new hat that Mac had ordered from the Western store.

Yesterday he'd gone to the cabin early and had gotten the roof up on the porch. Although he still had to tar paper and shingle it, at least it was nearly done.

Unfortunately, the work had nearly done him in. His back had screamed with pain by the time he knocked off work. But he'd then gone inside and sat with Madison for a little over an hour.

Once again he'd found it difficult to talk to her about her pregnancy and her apparently choosing to run away. Instead, they had talked about their jobs. He'd told her funny stories about the antics of his fellow cowboys when they'd been younger, and in turn she had told him funny stories about being a cashier at the grocery store.

The time had gone far too quickly and at least for that hour he'd forgotten his pain. The shared laughter had felt good and he hadn't wanted to get serious with her and steal away the bright sparkle in her beautiful eyes.

He parked in front of the Western store first. There were racks of clothing, a wall full of cowboy boots on display and another wall filled with hats in various shapes and colors.

"Hey, Flint." Russ Paxton, the owner of the store greeted him with a big smile.

"How's it going, Russ?" The two men shook hands.

"Sales have been a little slow. What about you? Couldn't you use a new pair of boots? And that hat you're wearing is looking pretty beat up. Don't you think it's about time for a new one?"

Flint laughed. "No, thanks, I'm good for now, Russ. I'm here to pick up a hat for Mac. He said you ordered one for him and called him the other day to tell him it was in."

"Indeed it is. I'll just go fetch it from the back." Russ turned and disappeared behind a curtained doorway.

The bell above the door tinkled and Flint turned to see Brad Ainsworth, Jim Browbeck and Zeke Osmond walk through the door. Flint nodded at Brad and Jim amicably, but had no such pleasantry for Zeke.

It was an odd group of men. Brad was the son of the mayor and had some political ambitions of his own. Jim was the well-liked chief of the volunteer fire department, and Zeke was a trouble-making ranch hand who worked for Raymond Humes, the man who owned the spread next to the Holiday Ranch.

"Hi, Flint," Jim said. "We're handing out fliers to everyone in town to announce a big bake sale next weekend at the community center."

"The funds will all go to the fire department. We all know the town needs another truck and hopefully we can raise enough money to see that goal accomplished," Brad said.

"Zeke, I didn't realize you were the charitable type," Flint said to the thin, dark-haired man who possessed weasel-like features.

"Chief Bowie thought it would be a good idea for me to help hand out fliers," Zeke replied, his gaze not quite meeting Flint's.

Flint wondered what Zeke had done to make Dillon give the man what sounded like a little community service. There was certainly no love lost between the men who worked for Raymond Humes and the men who worked for Cassie.

"Anyway, we're trying to get the word out about the event," Brad said.

"Here we are." Russ came out from the back room with a hatbox in his hand. He greeted the other men who handed him a dozen or so fliers to hand out to customers and then they left the shop.

"Mac already paid for the hat, so you're good to go…unless you want to replace that dusty old brown one you've got on your head," Russ said with a twinkle in his eyes.

Flint laughed. "You're a good salesman, Russ, but really I'm good for right now."

Moments later he carried the hatbox to his truck,

locked it up and then headed for the grocery store to pick up the things for Cookie.

As he walked he self-consciously touched the brim of his hat. He could use a new one, but what was the point? It wouldn't be long before he would no longer be a cowboy.

This thought stabbed a pain straight through his chest. If not a cowboy, then who was he? What was he? Sooner or later he was going to have to figure it out, but he shoved these troubling thoughts away for now.

After buying the land and the supplies for the cabin, he still had a nest egg left that would allow him to live for a year or so without doing much of anything. But he couldn't imagine being holed up in the cabin for a whole year without being productive.

It took him about forty-five minutes to shop and as Sherry Nielson, a pleasant middle-aged woman, checked him out, his brain immediately filled with thoughts of Madison.

He liked her. He liked her a lot. That surprised him. What surprised him even more was that despite knowing she was pregnant, he was extremely physically attracted to her.

He wanted to help her, but he didn't know how. Although most of the time she was cheerful and bright, there were times when dark shadows filled her eyes, shadows that spoke of bad things.

He wanted her to share those with him. He'd

never in his life wanted a woman to share her secrets with him, so what was so different about Madison?

He didn't know the answer to that, and in any case it didn't matter. Within a couple of days her car would be fixed and she'd be on her way.

When he arrived back at the ranch he pulled his truck around the cowboy motel to a back door that led into the kitchen area.

Cookie must have heard his approach as the man stood at the back door. The middle-aged man with his buzz-cut black hair and thickly muscled shoulders and arms looked more like a bodyguard than a man who loved to cook.

As usual, he wore no smile. Cookie had been at the ranch when Flint had first arrived. Flint had grown up with the man feeding him, but knew little more about him today than he had on the first day he'd met him.

"About time," Cookie said.

"I didn't dawdle too much," Flint replied wryly.

"Hmm." He began to grab the bags in the back of the truck, but before he did, Flint thought he caught a whisper of a smile from the taciturn man. Whenever one of the cowboys went to get supplies for Cookie, the man accused them of dawdling and taking too long.

It took only a few minutes to unload the groceries and then Flint headed for the stable where his duty for the day was shining up saddles and oiling up any leather paraphernalia. Thank goodness it was an easy job that wouldn't require him to use his back or knees.

In fact, lately he'd had a lot of days of being assigned to the easier chores around the ranch. He wondered if Sawyer knew the pain he was in or if it was just some sort of a coincidence?

Minutes later he was in the tack room in the stable. The scent of hay and horses and leather wrapped around him with both familiarity and comfort.

Big Cass had been a tough boss. From the very beginning she'd demanded the boys work hard and take pride in the jobs they accomplished. She could be stern at times, but she'd given her "boys" a sense of self-respect that had been lacking in each of the runaways. She'd also provided stability in their lives, a stability that had allowed them all to grow to their full potential.

Even though she could be stern, she could also be extremely loving. She became their mother figure and all of the men had deeply mourned her death.

He wasn't sure why he was thinking about her now. Maybe it was because he'd begun to mourn leaving this place, which had been home to him for so many years.

He had been working for about fifteen minutes

or so when Mac came in. "Hey, how's it going?" he asked.

Flint wiped his oily hands on a cloth and leaned against the workbench. "It's going. I've got your new hat in my room. Feel free to go in and grab it whenever you want."

"Thanks. I appreciate you picking it up for me."

"It was no problem. I was going into town to get supplies for Cookie anyway."

"How are things going at the cabin? You seem to be spending more time there in the evenings than usual."

Flint felt a rise of heat in his cheeks and hoped it wasn't evident to Mac. "I've got the porch up and I am in the process of shingling it."

"That's great. Once you have that done maybe you'll be back to spending the evenings with us in the rec room," Mac replied.

"Why, do you miss me?" Flint grinned at his friend.

"Nah, not me," Mac replied with his own grin. His smile faded and a small frown etched across his forehead. "Are you okay, Flint?"

He tensed. "Sure, I'm fine. Why do you ask?"

Mac shrugged. "You've just seemed kind of distant for the past couple of weeks or so."

"Distant? I haven't meant to be. I've just had a lot on my mind with the work at the cabin." The words were easy to say, but they weren't the whole truth.

Mac looked at him for a long minute. "You'd tell me if there was anything wrong, right? You know you can always talk to me, right?"

Flint laughed and clapped his friend on the back. "I know that, Mac. Really, I'm good so there's nothing for me to talk about. So what are you doing here anyway?"

"I'm about to start cleaning out stalls."

"Ah, so you drew one of the fun jobs for the day."

"Right, it's always been my idea of a fun time when I get to shovel out horse dung. I guess I'll get to it."

Minutes later he was once again alone and he thought about what Mac had said. Even before Madison had been in his cabin he *had* been distancing himself from the other men. He had to do that because sooner rather than later he would be leaving the Holiday Ranch and these men who had been constants in his life since he was thirteen years old.

Oh, he knew when he finally left here, the other men would promise to stay in touch and maybe for a couple of months they would, but ultimately Flint knew he'd wind up alone in that cabin with only his pain for company.

Mac, Flint and Jerod had developed strong friendships over the years. Although all twelve of the men who had grown up here were bonded, the three men had forged a deeper friendship together. He would miss their company most of all.

He cast off the depression that threatened to creep over him. There would be plenty of time for that later. Right now he was still a cowboy and he still worked on the Holiday Ranch.

And today Madison would probably hear from Larry Wright about her car and it was possible that by tomorrow she would be on her way. He was surprised that the idea of her leaving depressed him more than just a little bit.

It was odd and surprisingly pleasant to be greeted at the front door with her beautiful smile. He'd come to look forward to their evening visits and he was definitely concerned about her.

His concern was not only because he now knew she was a pregnant woman all on her own. And if that wasn't enough, he also suspected something terrible and violent might have happened to her. The thought of any man perpetrating violence on any woman surged a rich anger up inside him.

Had her boyfriend been abusive? Had he beaten her? Was he the one who had her so terrified all she could think about was leaving town? If that was the case then Flint would definitely like to know the name of the man responsible. But Madison wasn't giving anything up.

He didn't want to examine how his mood lifted later in the day when he left the ranch and headed for the cabin. When he pulled up front he was surprised when the door didn't open and Madison didn't appear.

Was it possible her car had been fixed and she had already left? Without even saying goodbye? He swallowed his disappointment. If that was the case then all that he could hope for was that wherever she went she would be safe and would find happiness. Even though he'd had very little time with her, he was surprised to realize he was definitely going to miss her.

The minute he opened the door he heard her. The sound of her sobbing came from the bedroom. What had happened? Had somebody found her here? His heart crashed against his ribs as he rushed toward the bedroom.

Chapter 4

"Madison, what's going on? Has somebody been here?"

Flint's deep voice penetrated Madison's sobs. She didn't know how long she'd been crying. She only knew her tears had begun after she'd hung up the phone after talking to Larry Wright at the garage.

"Madison, please tell me what's going on." He sat on the edge of the bed, his concern for her evident in the tone of his deep voice.

She sat up and drew several deep breaths in an attempt to stop the tears. She wiped her wet cheeks and looked miserably at Flint. "I got a call from Larry about my car. It needs a new m...m...motor and I don't have the m…money to fix it." The tears began to come again and her vision blurred with the watery display.

There was no way she could afford to fix her car. There was no way she could return to her trailer. She couldn't take advantage of Flint any longer and she didn't know what she was going to do. All she felt at the moment was a deep despair.

"Madison, I can loan you the money to fix your car," Flint offered.

His kindness only made her cry more. She couldn't take his money to fix her car. She wouldn't even consider it. He'd done more than enough for her already.

"Madison, you need to stop crying. It's not good for you."

"I'm not taking any money from you," she replied. His generosity to a virtual stranger was one of the reasons she liked him. "This isn't your problem, Flint. I'm not your problem." She scooted down to the end of the bed to stand as he also rose to his feet. Together they went into the living room where she sank down on the sofa, exhausted by all the tears she'd shed.

"So what are you going to do?" he asked.

Dear Lord, she wished she had a good answer. "I'll figure something out, although I would appreciate it if I could stay here one more night and then I'll be on my way."

She attempted to smile at him with a forced confidence. Inside she was terrified. Maybe she should just take a bus out of town and ride it until the end of the line. Wherever she landed she'd somehow have to figure out how to make things work.

"Of course you can stay another night," he replied. "But what's one more night going to do to fix your situation?"

The smile she'd tried to force fell away. "I don't know," she replied in a mere whisper. "I'll just get to a bus station in the morning and…and…"

"And what? Try to start a new life in a new place without a car?" He was silent for several long moments. "I'll tell you what," he finally said. "I have a deal to offer you."

"What kind of a deal?" she asked and eyed him suspiciously.

"You stay here and take care of the cleaning and cook me dinner every night and I'll pay you a salary. Before you know it you'll have earned the money for the car repairs."

She stared at him skeptically. "And all I have to do is clean up around here and cook you meals?" Was this the beginning of Flint showing another side of himself to her?

"I swear that's it, nothing else. Although I wouldn't mind if you'd open up a little with me and tell me who the baby's father is and why you aren't with him."

"Flint, I really don't want to talk about that, but if you're serious about that deal then I'll take it as long as you agree not to tell anyone I'm here." For the first time since the phone call from the car shop a small nugget of hope rose up in her chest. Despite not knowing him for very long, she realized she'd trusted him.

She knew he had offered her the deal out of the kindness of his heart. The cabin certainly didn't need daily cleaning and he could take his meals on the ranch with the other men. This was a way for her to earn her keep and hold on to her dignity. But she knew he didn't need this service.

Still, if he wanted to pretend that he did need her and pay her for her efforts, then she would be the best darned cleaner and cook he'd ever known. And she would forever be grateful to him.

"Then, it's a deal," he said and held out his hand for her to shake. "I'll bring some more groceries in tomorrow and I'll start eating dinner here with you."

She grabbed his hand and shook it solemnly. "Thank you, Flint." Tears burned at her eyes once again.

He cleared his throat. "Okay, I'm heading outside to get some work done. I'll see you in a little while."

The minute he walked out the door she broke down again, this time with gratefulness to whatever powers that had brought her Flint McCay. She didn't even want to think about what would have happened to her if somebody else had found her hiding out in the Holiday barn.

She had no idea what he was going to pay her, but she knew he would be generous. It might take her months to get enough money for the car repairs, but as long as nobody knew she was here at least she would be safe. And that sense of safety was so important to her.

Someday when she was away from Bitterroot and settled with a new life and a new job, she would send monthly checks to Flint until she paid off her debt to him. Of course, she could never repay him for his kindness and support at this, the lowest point in her entire life.

Hopefully, when it came time to give birth to her baby she would be someplace safe and she could build a healthy and loving home for them. She loved the baby growing inside her and she was determined to be the best mother she could be.

She moved to the window and looked outside where Flint was unloading bundles of shingles from the back of his truck. He didn't have his hat on and the waning sunshine sparkled in his slightly shaggy, but beautiful blond hair.

She saw the grimace that crossed his features after he placed one of the bundles on the ground. He leaned against the truck for several long moments.

This wasn't the first time she'd thought she'd seen pain twisting his features.

Had he pulled some muscles? Was he pushing himself too hard working on the ranch all day long and then coming out here to do more physical work? Should he be the one to see a doctor?

She turned away from the window. This was none of her business. Even though she was living in his cabin and would be cooking his meals, that didn't mean he was inviting her into his personal life.

Still, she couldn't help the way her heart lifted when he knocked off work and came in to have a cup of coffee with her. "I should be able to finish up with the front porch tomorrow evening," he said as he took his seat at the table.

"That's good." She set the coffee before him and then sat across from him. "Maybe now you can relax a bit in the evenings rather than working so hard."

He smiled. "Not quite yet. I still need to finish up the garage."

"You're a hard worker, Flint," she observed.

"I like being productive. So tell me, Madison Taylor, can you cook?"

"Absolutely. I started cooking for my father when I was about eight, right after my mother passed away. He wanted full meat and potato meals, not boxed mac and cheese and a hot dog."

"So what's your specialty?"

She frowned thoughtfully. "I'd probably have to say my smothered steak with cheesy mashed potatoes."

"Hmm, sounds good." His green eyes shone with a warmth that enveloped her. That warmth, the caring she felt emanating from him, was becoming something she craved. At this moment with the last gasp of daylight filtering in through the nearby window, she felt completely at ease and protected. It felt so good after the last couple months of hell.

"Are you a picky eater?" she asked. If she was really going to do this deal with him, then she wanted to make sure she cooked him the absolute best meals he could ever eat. "Do you have things you absolutely won't eat?"

"I'm definitely not a picky eater, but there are two things I don't want to see on my plate...sushi and tofu. I like my seafood cooked and that tofu stuff is just not right."

She laughed. "Actually, I'm in agreement about those two foods. I think they're both gross." She sobered. "Flint, eventually I will repay you for everything, but I'll never be able to repay you for your kindness to me. We both know you don't need me here cooking and cleaning, that you just made up this job to help me out. You're my own special kind of angel and I can't ever thank you enough."

His gaze held hers for a long moment and then

he looked down into his coffee cup. He cleared his throat and gazed at her once again.

"Madison, trust me. I'm no angel. I need to start spending more time here. Sooner rather than later I'm going to be living here full-time. So you're actually helping me out here and I don't want to talk about this arrangement again. It's a done deal." He smiled, that beautiful smile of his that once again shot a rivulet of heat through her.

"So when you move in here full-time are you still going to work on the Holiday Ranch?"

"No." A frown raced quickly across his forehead.

"Then what are you going to do?" she asked curiously.

His eyes darkened and shuttered and once again he looked down into his coffee. She realized she'd probably overstepped. "I'm sorry. It's really none of my business," she said hurriedly.

"No, you're fine. The problem is I'm not sure what I'm going to do. All I know is that I'm tired of what I'm doing right now and it's time for a change."

There was something in his eyes, something in his voice, that made her not quite believe him. She had a feeling she wasn't the only one who had secrets.

He left the cabin soon after with the promise to return around noon the next day with a list of groceries she'd written out for him. She'd always loved cooking and she was actually looking forward to cooking for him.

The morning had started so badly with the call from Larry about her car, but as she got ready for bed that night she was almost glad it was going to take a while to get the car fixed.

Flint pulled up in front of the cabin and instantly his appetite came to life. For the past four days Madison had cooked dinner for him and she was definitely one hell of a cook.

As important as the meal they shared was the conversation between them. In a million years Flint wouldn't have imagined that he'd spend time with a woman who was so easy to talk to, so easy to share laughter with. In a million years he never would have guessed that there would be a woman he felt so at ease with.

However, he had to admit that there were moments when she stirred more than an edge of desire in him that was distinctly not comfortable. The last thing he wanted to do was take advantage of her.

They had talked about food and politics, about favorite television shows and music. But what she had not discussed was her fear and the baby's father.

He now got out of his truck and tried not to notice the sweet anticipation that swept through him as he thought of seeing Madison again.

Before he got to the door it opened and she stood

in the threshold with that beautiful smile of hers that warmed him from head to toe. "Hi," she said.

"Hi, yourself," he replied.

"I hope you brought your appetite." She smiled.

"Always."

She stepped aside to let him in. As he swept past her he caught the familiar scent of her wildflower fragrance. It whirled around in his head, half dizzying him with a not altogether unpleasant tension.

"How was your day?" she asked as she gestured him to a chair at the table.

"Not too bad," he replied, although that wasn't exactly the truth. The day had been cloudy and gray with thunderstorms in the forecast for later in the evening.

On days like these his pain level was particularly high and he really had to push to get through the chores. At least now he could get off his feet for a spell and relax for the rest of the evening.

"Something smells good," he observed.

"Chicken fried steak with mashed potatoes and gravy." She pulled two plates from the cabinet and filled them, adding a side of corn and warm biscuits.

"You're spoiling me," he said once she joined him at the table.

"Nonsense. I enjoy cooking for you. There's nothing more depressing than cooking for one and eating all alone. I've spent most of my adult life eating all alone so I'm enjoying this."

Once again he found himself curious about her story. Had she had a relationship with the father of her baby? Had they been dating? Or was the pregnancy a result of a one-night stand and she was simply too embarrassed to admit such a thing?

Flint considered himself one of the most non-judgmental men he knew. Growing up as one of Cass Holiday's "lost boys," he'd received plenty of "judgment" from the other boys and even some of the adults in town.

Homeless trash. Runaway rats. Cass's creeps. Those were just a few of the things the boys in town would yell at the boys from the Holiday Ranch. Nobody said those kinds of things to them anymore. They had proven themselves over the years to be good, upstanding citizens in town.

"So how was your day?" he now asked her.

"It was okay," she said after a moment of hesitation.

"But…"

"But what?" She looked at him curiously.

"I don't know. You said your day was okay but I sensed a *but* at the end of your sentence."

She grinned at him. "You're very astute." Her grin fell away and she glanced toward the nearby window. "I really hate thunderstorms."

"I'm not particularly fond of them myself," he

replied. "But it's been so hot and dry lately and we all could really use the rain."

She gazed toward the window once again and shadows darkened her eyes…shadows that whispered of fear. "Maybe I'll just stick around here until the storm passes," he said.

She looked at him once again and smiled softly. "You don't have to do that, Flint. I'm a big girl and I'll survive a thunderstorm."

"We'll see." He knew she already lived with some kind of fear. If a storm made her even more afraid and he could alleviate some of that fear, then why wouldn't he stick around until the storm passed? Any man would make the same choice.

His decision had nothing to do with the fact that when she gazed at him a certain way he felt like a better man than what he was. It had nothing to do with the way her smile warmed him from head to toe and that there were moments when he fantasized about kissing her enticing lips.

As usual the meal was delicious and the conversation remained light and easy. He helped her clean up the dishes and then they moved to the sofa for more conversation.

He couldn't help but notice that in the long summer dress she wore, her pregnancy was beginning to show. Although it did nothing to detract from her attractiveness, it was a reminder to him that his physical feelings toward her were way out of line.

"You haven't gotten sick the past couple of nights," he said.

"I know. I guess the morning sickness has finally passed."

"So overall how are you feeling?"

"Actually, really good."

"Isn't it time you see a doctor?"

The sparkle in her eyes dimmed. "I can't. There's no way I'm seeing a doctor here in Bitterroot. Besides, the only thing he'd probably tell me at this point is that I need some prenatal vitamins."

"Is that something I could get for you?"

"I'm not sure, but I imagine the drugstore might have them, but I wouldn't want anyone to see you buying them and figuring out somehow that you're buying them for me." Her eyes once again took on a dark haunting that reminded him that she had secrets…secrets so bad she didn't want anyone to know her location.

He frowned thoughtfully. "I can't imagine how anyone would be able to connect the two of us. I'll see about getting them from the drugstore for you tomorrow. I'll put on my glasses with the fake nose and bushy black eyebrows and nobody will recognize me."

She laughed, the musical sound warming his heart. "Please tell me you don't really have glasses with a fake nose attached."

He grinned. "Okay, I don't really have glasses

with a fake nose, but if the pharmacy has prenatal vitamins, I'll pick you up some tomorrow." He was grateful to see her eyes clear and bright once again.

"Thank you. I'd appreciate it. Then I know the baby is getting what he or she needs." A crash of distant thunder punctuated her sentence and she released a small cry.

"Hey, it's okay," he said. "It's just a couple of clouds banging together. Thunder can't hurt you."

"Logically, I know that." She offered him a tentative smile.

"Have you always been afraid of storms?" he asked.

"Not always." Her gaze skittered away from his. "It's just been in the past couple of months. Would you like a cup of coffee?"

It was an obvious attempt to change the subject. "No, thanks, I'm good. So what else did you do today besides cook me a great meal?"

"I watched a little television and then read for a while."

"And from the cover of the book I've seen you reading you must like those romance novels?" Another boom of thunder sounded and she nodded. "What do you like about those books?" Maybe if he kept her engaged in conversation she wouldn't notice that the storm was moving closer.

"One of the reasons I like them is because I love happy endings and that's what you always get with a romance novel. I also like that in them you see people struggle and overcome all kinds of problems. When I close the book at the end, I always have hope that there's going to be a happy ending for me." She blushed and he found it all utterly charming.

"And what would look like a happy ending for you?"

She offered him a wistful smile as her eyes took on a soft glow. "Someday I'd like to be married to a cowboy who loves me and my child to distraction. I'd want maybe one or two more babies to build the big, loving family I never really had."

Well, that certainly let him out. Not that he planned on being in her future, but if she wanted a cowboy, in a month or two he would no longer be that. He wasn't sure what he'd be.

Lightning illuminated the room, followed by a boom of thunder that shook the rafters. Madison jumped up off the sofa, her eyes holding the same wild look she'd had on the first day when he'd awakened her from her nap and she'd had the knife in her hand.

"Is the door locked?" She rushed to the front door and locked it, then slammed her back against it. As thunder sounded again she cried out and looked frantically at Flint.

"Don't...don't let him in. Please, help me to keep him out." She began to sob.

"Madison..." Flint got up and went to her. He took one of her trembling hands in his and pulled her away from the door. "Nobody is getting in. Honey, you're safe here."

He guided her to the sofa and they sat. He put his arm around her and pulled her against his side. He had so many questions, but at the moment all he wanted to do was ease her fear. She burrowed into him, her body trembling uncontrollably.

"You're okay, Madison. I'm right here beside you and I won't let anyone hurt you." Rain pelted the window, and thunder sounded once again.

She buried her head against his chest and squeezed her eyes tightly closed. He rubbed her shoulder in an effort to calm her. "Thunder is nothing but the angels bowling," he said. "Once in a while they just need a little downtime and so they get out of their white robes and half of them dress in blue bowling shirts and the other half dress in red bowling shirts. They check their wings and their harps at the door and then start the bowling. It makes a lot of noise down here, but you have to admit they deserve to have a little fun now and then in their lives."

He was relieved to hear a small giggle escape her. She raised her head and gazed at him. Her lush lips were mere inches from his and for just a brief moment he forgot how to breathe. All he wanted was to taste her lips.

Thunder sounded once again and the moment was broken as she shot a glance at the door. It was then that Flint realized she wasn't afraid of the thunder. She was afraid of something that had happened to her while it was thundering. Somebody had hurt her. Somebody had hurt her badly and he definitely wanted to know what had happened.

"Madison, what happened to you when it was storming? Please tell me."

She reared away from him and her eyes once again held a wildness that easily rivaled the storm overhead. "I c…c…can't tell. I…can't."

"Yes, you can. All your secrets are safe with me, Madison. Please, tell me what happened to you."

She stared at him for a long moment. "It was lightning and…and thundering and…and I…he… he beat me…and then…and then he…he raped me." Her voice was a mere whisper, but they screamed inside Flint's head. Beaten? Raped?

Tears brimmed in her eyes and then fell down her cheeks as she continued to gaze at him. "I… I was raped, Flint. And my rapist is the father of my baby."

Chapter 5

Why had she told him? Oh, God, she shouldn't have told. She shouldn't have ever told. She had never intended to tell anyone. Now Flint would look at her differently. He'd feel differently about her.

She jumped up from the sofa and turned her back on Flint. She didn't want to see his disgust for her in his eyes. Just thinking about what had happened to her made her feel so dirty and ugly.

The memories of that horrible night mentally pummeled her and even though she felt like crying all over again, she sucked in a deep breath to staunch any further tears. She'd shed enough tears and crying changed nothing. She'd been beaten and raped and now she was pregnant with her rapist's child. She steeled herself and then turned back to look at him.

"My God, Madison. How did it happen? Who did this to you?"

Thankfully, she saw no judgment in his eyes, only a stunned shock. She drew in a deep breath and released it slowly. "It happened a little over three months ago. It was storming and I was driving home after work. I'd gotten about halfway home when my stupid car broke down."

She was grateful that her voice held none of the emotion that boiled and churned inside her. "He drove up and asked me if I needed a ride home. I knew I couldn't get the car running again and I knew him from around town and he had a good reputation, so I agreed to the ride."

She stared at a spot just over Flint's head. She remembered the rain that had pelted the car window, the wipers swishing back and forth and the lightning that had split the night sky. Thunder had boomed overhead, but he'd been so nice and she was immediately put at ease.

Her throat constricted as she once again gazed at Flint, and the memories continued to assault her. "He was so nice and all I wanted was a ride home. When we got to my trailer he insisted that he walk me to the door because he had an umbrella to shield me from the rain. So he walked me to the door and when we got there he shoved his way inside and began to beat me."

She raised a hand to her face, remembering his fists slamming into her and the excruciating pain of each blow. "He liked it…he liked hitting me. It…it made him excited. He laughed while I was moaning in pain. And then…and then he raped me."

Her breath caught in the back of her throat. She drew a deep breath and then continued, "I thought it was done…that he…he would never bother me again after that night, but I was wrong."

"He came back?" Flint's voice was soft.

She gave a curt nod as her emotions once again threatened to get away from her. "He came back the night before you found me in your barn. But that night I barred my door. I moved every piece of furniture I owned in front of the door and he banged and banged on it. It was like the thunder from the first time he'd gotten inside was back and I was so afraid that he'd manage to get in, but eventually he went away."

"Who, Madison? Who did this?"

She ignored his question. "I knew the only way to assure that he would never touch me again was to leave Bitterroot. Besides, the last thing I wanted him to know was that I was pregnant with his baby. He would try to take the baby away from me. So I spent the next day packing up my car with everything I thought I would need to start over someplace else. And then my car broke down and here I am."

Flint gestured for her to rejoin him on the sofa. She suddenly realized the storm that had been overhead had passed and the only sound she could hear was the frantic beating of her own heart.

She sank down on the sofa next to Flint and wrapped her arms around her stomach. "That's why I told you this baby has no father. No matter how I conceived, I love this baby growing inside me."

"Madison, please tell me who beat you and raped you. Tell me his name." Flint's eyes were glazed with a hard glint she'd never seen before.

She shook her head. "It doesn't matter who he is. He'll never get the opportunity to hurt me again. And even if I did tell you his name, you wouldn't believe me."

That was what he'd told her when he was beating her...that nobody would ever believe her if she told. He had all the power and she was just a stupid checker at the grocery store who lived in a cheap trailer park. And someplace in the very depths of her heart she'd believed him. Nobody would ever believe her.

"Try me, Madison. I would believe anything you tell me," he replied.

"I can't, Flint. I won't. Just leave it alone now." The wild emotions that had raced through her were gone, leaving her utterly exhausted. "But I need you to know I didn't flirt with him. I didn't lead him on in any way. All I wanted was a ride home in the rain."

His gaze softened. "Oh, Madison, that thought never even crossed my mind. I… I can't even find the words. I'm just so damned sorry you had to go through that." He reached out and took one of her hands in his. "You definitely didn't deserve what happened to you."

Even though someplace in her mind she'd known that, she hadn't realized just how much she'd needed to hear it from somebody else. Tears shimmered in her vision. "Thank you, Flint," she said softly.

"You know, you should probably talk to somebody…maybe a therapist. You know Ellie Miller is a psychologist here in town. I think you definitely have a little PTSD."

"Maybe, but I won't talk to anyone in Bitterroot." She sighed. "I'm just really tired right now and I'm sure you're exhausted, too. The storms have stopped and I just want to go to sleep."

She stood. Although the last thing she wanted was to be alone with her memories, she really was depleted by reliving it all just now. All she wanted to do now was forget it all and fall into a deep, dreamless sleep.

He stood, his gaze intense on her. "Are you sure you don't want to tell me his name?"

"Yes, I'm sure. Besides, it doesn't matter now.

It's over and done and hopefully I'll never have to see his face again." She walked him to the door, although she could tell he was reluctant to leave her alone. "You don't have to worry about me, Flint. I'll be fine for the rest of the night."

He stopped at the door and turned back to face her. He reached out and gently dragged his fingers down the side of her face. "You aren't in this alone anymore, Madison." He leaned forward and kissed her cheek.

She wanted to turn her head so his lips captured hers, but she didn't. And in any case his gentle kiss only lasted a moment and then he was gone.

Madison locked the door after him and then went into her bedroom. She was oddly relieved by telling Flint what had happened to her. She'd lived with the pain and the horror of it for a little over three long months, and sharing it had eased some of her pain, but certainly not all of it.

It had taken weeks for her bruises to fade and for her body pain to heal from the beating he'd given her. It would take her a lot longer to forget the abject horror she'd felt on that night.

She knew eventually she probably needed to talk to somebody professional to deal with the emotional issues the attack had left behind. She had terrible nightmares about it far too often.

She hadn't lied to Flint when she told him she loved her baby. She'd been appalled when she'd first discovered she was pregnant. However, she'd quickly been able to separate the innocent life she carried from the evil man who had been part of creating it.

She changed her clothes and got into bed. Even though she'd wanted to immediately fall asleep, her thoughts went right to that moment when Flint had touched her face and the sweet kiss he'd given her on her cheek.

It surprised her how much she wished he'd given her a real kiss on the lips. She'd wanted him to wrap his big, strong arms around her and kiss her until he found every cold spot inside her and warmed them.

Oh yes, the desire she had for him surprised her. She'd worried that she would never feel that way for a man again. Her rapist might have taken a lot away from her, but apparently, he hadn't taken away her ability to want a kind and gentle man like Flint.

She had to keep reminding herself that this cabin was just a temporary resting place. More important, she had to remember that Flint was just being kind to her and he couldn't be anyone important to her.

Even knowing that, he felt like somebody important. And he was getting more important to her each day that they spent time together.

This felt like home when he arrived each evening for dinner. He felt like home when they ate together and talked and laughed.

But he couldn't be the cowboy she wanted. He

couldn't be the man who would give her a romance novel's happy ending because her happy ending could never happen in Bitterroot.

It was just after noon the next day when Flint entered the drugstore to see about buying Madison her prenatal vitamins. He'd spent most of the night tossing and turning as he'd replayed over and over again what Madison had told him.

He wanted the name of the man who had hurt her…the man who had beaten and raped her. If he had the name, then he would hunt him down and beat the hell out of him. At the very least the man needed to be arrested and prosecuted to the fullest extent of the law.

He couldn't imagine the horror and the pain that Madison had experienced at the hand of a man. The terror he'd seen in her eyes haunted him. No wonder she'd greeted him with a butcher knife when she hadn't really known anything about him. If she slept with a knife beneath her mattress every day for the rest of her life he would understand.

The fact that some man who lived in Bitterroot had done this to any woman enraged him. Who? Who had done this terrible thing? Who, in Bitterroot, was hiding this kind of sick madness inside him?

He was hoping that Madison would trust him with the man's name, but he realized that might take a little time. He was just grateful she'd trusted him enough to tell him what she had.

He now walked up the vitamin aisle in the drugstore and froze as he saw Mabel McAllistar standing there. Mabel was part of a group of older women who were retired from their jobs, but worked full-time at gossiping.

"Hello, Flint," she said.

"Mrs. McAllistar." He tipped his hat to her.

"I'm in here looking for something for good colon health. Are you looking for anything in particular?" Her beady brown eyes gazed at him with open curiosity.

"I…uh…think I might have a little poison ivy and so I'm looking for something for the itch."

"You have a rash? Let me see it and I can tell you if it's poison ivy."

"Ma'am, in order to show you the itch I'd have to drop my drawers," Flint replied.

"Oh, my." A blush covered her cheeks. "Well, we can't have that, now, can we? My George gets poison ivy almost every summer. Let me show you the cream that works best for him." To Flint's surprise she grabbed him by the arm and pulled him down the next aisle.

"This really isn't necessary," he protested. "I could find something myself."

"Nonsense. We don't want you itching and feeling miserable because you bought the wrong brand," she replied. She stopped in front of the medicated creams section and scanned the boxes and bottles. "Ah, here it is. You'd better get the big bottle so you have plenty. You know how easily poison ivy spreads." She grabbed the bottle off the shelf and handed it to him.

"Thank you." He took the bottle from her and then he headed for the cashier and paid. He left the pharmacy, but didn't go far. There was no way he could buy any prenatal vitamins while Mabel was in the store.

He needed to wait until she left and then he'd go back inside and get what Madison needed. He walked a short distance down the sidewalk and then leaned back against the grocery store building. From this vantage point he would be able to see when Mabel left the drugstore, and hopefully she wouldn't see him.

He straightened as he saw Brad Ainsworth and his close friend Charlie Kudrow headed in his direction. Flint didn't really know the mayor's son that well, although he knew he worked as an insurance agent. Charlie was a big animal veterinarian and had been out to the ranch on more than one occasion when a cow or horse was ill or injured.

"Hey, Flint," Charlie greeted him with smile.

"Brad… Charlie," Flint replied.

"What are you doing just hanging out on the street?" Charlie asked.

"Just taking a moment to enjoy the sunshine after the storms last night," Flint replied.

"We're headed to the café for some lunch. You want to join us?" Brad asked.

"Thanks, but I need to get back to the ranch in just a little while." Out of the corner of his eye he saw Mabel leave the pharmacy. "But thanks for the invite."

The minute the two men disappeared into the café's front door, Flint hurried back inside the pharmacy. He searched the shelves but didn't find any prenatal vitamins. He finally headed to the back where the owner and head pharmacist Ed Parker stood behind a counter.

"Flint, I was wondering when you were going to show up to get that prescription I've been holding for you," Ed said.

"Actually, I'm not here about that." It had been a little over three weeks ago since Flint had received a diagnosis and the doctor had written him a prescription, but somehow in his mind if he didn't pick up the meds, then he didn't have the disease.

"I need some prenatal vitamins, but I didn't see them on the shelf," he said.

"Ah, I believe I have some back here. Just give me a minute." Ed disappeared behind a shelving unit.

Flint turned to look around, wanting to make sure nobody was there to see or hear what he was

getting. After Madison's confession the night before there was absolutely no way he wanted anyone to be able to connect her to him. He now knew
the reason for her fear and it was vital she remain
a secret at his cabin and thankfully, he knew Ed
didn't gossip.

"Here we are," Ed said as he returned with a
large bottle of the vitamins. "Do you want to pay
for these back here?"

"That would be great. Thanks, Ed."

"I'll add in the cost of your prescription, too." He
told Flint the cost and minutes later Flint left the
pharmacy. He tossed his own prescription into his
glove box and left the poison ivy cream and the vitamins in a bag on his passenger seat. It was crazy;
he now had a prescription he didn't want to think
about and a bottle of poison ivy medicine he didn't
need, but at least he had gotten Madison's vitamins.

As he headed back to the ranch his thoughts once
again returned to Madison and what she'd told him
the night before. Somehow, he had to make her trust
him enough to give him the name of the man who
had assaulted her.

Whoever he was, he needed to be brought to justice. He was a violent predator and it was quite possible he was preying on other vulnerable women in
town. Besides, he needed to be put into jail for what
he did to Madison. His fingers tightened around the

steering wheel with anger. The man needed to burn in hell for what he had done to Madison.

He pulled into the ranch and parked his truck in the shed, and then headed for the dining room where he knew the other cowboys were probably close to finishing up their lunch.

When he got there he grabbed a plate and filled it even as Cookie was starting to clear off the buffet. "Where have you been?" Mac asked him as he sat next to him at one of the tables.

"I had a few errands to run in town," Flint replied.

Mac eyed him long and hard. "What's going on with you?"

"What do you mean?" Flint realized most of the other men had finished up and left the dining room. Mac's plate was empty but it was obvious he wasn't going anywhere until he got some answers from Flint.

"You know what I mean. You disappear during the days at odd times and you've even stopped eating dinner here with all of us. We never see you in the evenings anymore. I thought the cabin was just a weekend getaway and someplace you would retire to when that time came. So if that's the case then why are you spending so much time there now?"

Flint stared down at the sandwich on his plate and then looked back at his friend. "I'm seriously considering quitting my job here."

Mac's eyebrows rose as he looked at Flint in stunned surprise. "Now? Why?"

"I'm just ready for a change." Flint hated lying to his good friend, but he didn't want anyone to know the real reason he had to quit. He didn't want to see the pity that might appear in their eyes.

"But what are you going to do?"

"I don't know yet," Flint replied. "I just know my time here is coming to an end."

"So the cabin is going to be your new home soon?"

Flint nodded. "It's got everything I need."

"I'll be honest. I'm glad for you if this is really what you want, but everyone on the ranch is going to miss you," Mac said. "I'm going to miss you."

Flint smiled despite knowing how difficult it was going to be for him to tell everyone goodbye. "It isn't like I'm dying or moving a thousand miles away. We'll still see each other around town and anytime you want to take me to dinner at the café, as long as you're paying I'll be there." Flint wanted to put a lighter tone to the conversation.

Mac laughed. "Yeah, I know that's right and you'd probably ask for the most expensive item on the menu."

Flint grinned at him. "Yeah, I probably would."

"On that note I guess I'd better shut up and let you eat your lunch." Mac stood. "So how much longer will you be here?"

"I don't know. I'm taking it day by day right now and I'd rather you not mention it to anyone else. I don't want anyone to know until I've had a chance to talk to Cassie."

Minutes later Flint was alone in the dining room. He ate his lunch quickly and then headed for the stables where his job for the rest of the day was to muck out the horse stalls.

As he worked his thoughts continued to play and replay what Madison had told him about the attack on her. He didn't think her keeping it a secret was good for anyone. The perpetrator needed to be arrested both for Madison's sake and for the sake of any other woman he might go after.

At five o'clock he was back in his truck and headed for the cabin and Madison. There was no question he was developing feelings for her, feelings that confused him because he'd never felt them before.

Certainly, he felt a protectiveness over her and he enjoyed her company a lot. But there was a simmer inside him, a simmer that whispered of something exciting and raw each time he got too close to her. However, he knew he had to keep a lid on it, that it was totally inappropriate considering their circumstances.

In any case she wasn't going to be particularly happy with him tonight because he intended to press her hard for the name of her attacker.

There was no way it was right for her to have to leave Bitterroot, to leave her home, because some pervert had attacked her. He was the one who had done wrong, so why was she the one facing terrible and life-changing consequences?

He wanted the name so they could turn him into Dillon Bowie, the chief of police. Dillon was a no-nonsense lawman who would get the attacker behind bars. Then she wouldn't have to leave Bitterroot.

As usual when he pulled up in front of the cabin, she stepped out on the front porch to greet him. And as usual, the sight of her warmed him. She was clad in another one of her sleeveless dresses, this one a spring yellow that looked lovely with her dark hair.

It was after another delicious dinner and when they were side by side on the sofa when he finally broached the difficult subject. "Madison, we need to have a serious talk," he began.

Instantly, a wariness leaped into her eyes and a frown line danced across her forehead. "I don't like the sound of that."

He took one of her hands in his as he gazed into her bright blue eyes. "I want the name of your rapist."

She yanked her hand from his and shook her head. She actually scowled at him. "I don't want to have this discussion."

"Madison, you need to hear me out. He needs to be brought to justice."

"I told you to just leave it alone, Flint. I already told you more than I ever intended telling anyone."

"I can't leave it alone. When I think of what he did to you, my blood boils."

Her gaze softened. "Another reason not to tell you his name. The last thing I want is for you to go off and do something stupid and then you wind up in jail."

"As much as I'd love to beat the hell out of him, I promise you that won't happen. I want you to go into Dillon's office and make an official report of what happened to you."

She grabbed hold of his forearm and squeezed it. "Don't you understand? Didn't you listen to what I told you? Nobody will ever believe me."

"That's not true, Madison. I'll believe you... Dillon will believe you." He could tell she was still completely shut down by the darkness in her eyes and the stiffness of her body next to his.

"Madison, I can protect you from him," he said. "I swear I won't let anyone hurt you, but turning him in is the right thing to do."

She jumped off the sofa, her body positively vibrating as she glared at him. "It's easy for you to talk about what the right thing is to do. You weren't the one beaten up and violated. He didn't come to your door and try to barge in so that he could do it to you all over again."

"You're right. I can't even pretend to imagine what that was like for you. But I worry that while he's still out walking the streets he's preying on other women," he replied.

She suddenly looked stricken and her face paled. "I never thought about that," she whispered. "I never thought about there being others."

Tears began to fall down her cheeks. Flint's instinct was to get up and go to her, to comfort her, but he didn't move from the sofa. She needed to decide what she was going to do without any more input from him. He'd spoken his truth and now it was up to her.

She swiped at her tears and closed her eyes, her features tortured by whatever was going through her mind. She finally opened her eyes and her lips trembled. "Brad," she whispered. "It was Brad Ainsworth."

He stared at her in stunned surprise. Of all the men in town, the son of the mayor, the man who hoped to fill his father's office when he retired, was the very last man he would have thought to be guilty of this.

Brad was well liked, well respected, by everyone in Bitterroot, but apparently the man had a very dark side that he managed to keep hidden in his day-to-day activities. The man was a monster.

Flint got up off the sofa and went to her. He pulled her into his arms and held her close as she began to cry once again. "Thank you, Madison," he said softly. "Thank you for trusting me with this. Now we're going to get him arrested and where he can never hurt another woman again."

She leaned away and looked up at him. "I'm scared, Flint. I believe he's dangerous and the very personification of evil."

"All the more reason to get him off the streets," he said.

He pulled her back against him and he patted her back reassuringly even though a touch of apprehension swept through him. As soon as they made an official report, they would find out just how dangerous Brad Ainsworth might be.

In the meantime, Flint was determined to keep her safe; he just hoped his efforts to that end were enough.

Chapter 6

At ten o'clock the next morning Madison stood at the cabin's front door waiting for Flint to show up. Her stomach rolled with nausea and her palms were damp. Her breath hitched in her chest with anxiety.

Flint should be here at any moment and then they were going to Chief Bowie's office so she could report what Brad Ainsworth had done to her.

She felt half-sick with apprehension. What if Dillon didn't believe her? What if word got out around Bitterroot and nobody believed her? In the eyes of the rest of the town Brad was a likeable, upstanding citizen. But she knew the truth about him. She knew the very darkness of his soul.

There was no question that she was scared, but she had to admit to herself that there had been a bit of relief in telling Flint who was responsible for the attack. She'd held this inside for over three long months.

Flint had promised her he'd keep her safe and that there would be no way Brad could trace her to the cabin, but she wasn't sure how he intended to accomplish that. He was the one taking her to see Dillon and certainly word would get out about him being the one who was helping her.

And the idea that Brad would know she was here all alone made her want to pack her bags and somehow escape. She rested a hand on her belly. Her pregnancy was definitely beginning to show and that scared her, as well. The last thing she wanted was for Brad to know on that night of violence against her he had fathered a child.

She moved her hand from her belly to her forehead where a stress headache was beginning to pound. There was no question that she was scared. But she was also tired of being scared and hopefully justice would prevail, Brad would go to jail and she'd never, ever have to be afraid again. She had to believe it would happen that way. She desperately needed to believe it.

A rumble of approaching vehicles sounded in the distance. She was expecting Flint, but it sounded like more than one truck coming. She went to the front door and opened it.

Surprise shot through her as Flint's truck came into view, followed by half a dozen other trucks. They filled the clearing in front of the cabin. What the heck…?

Flint got out of his truck and approached her. "I hope you aren't angry with me," he said.

"What's going on?" Whoever was with him now knew she was here in the cabin. Oh, God, she was no longer a secret. Her anxiety level soared off the charts. "Flint, for goodness' sake, what are all these others doing here?"

"I told some of the other men at the ranch what was going on. I swear they will keep your location a secret here, but this was the safest way to get you to the police station without anyone being able to figure out exactly where you're staying and who is helping you."

She wanted to be angry with him for breaking her confidence, but she knew whatever he had done, whomever he had told, ultimately she had to believe that he had her best interest at heart.

"These men won't tell anyone that you're here. I'd trust them with my life," Flint said.

"So why are they all here?" She looked beyond Flint's broad shoulder to the variety of trucks.

"They're all coming with us to the police station. I don't want you riding into town with me. Instead,

I want you to ride with Mac McBride. You know him, right?"

"He's come through my line at the grocery store before. He's always seemed nice."

"He's a terrific guy, like all the men I brought with me are. If we all go into the police station together, then Brad won't know who, specifically, is helping you."

A shiver of apprehension swept through her. What she wanted to do now was tell everyone to just forget it, that she'd changed her mind about going to report the crime. But Flint had obviously gone to a lot of trouble to make this work this morning, and then she thought of Brad possibly preying on other young women and her resolve to do the right thing returned.

"Let's go," she said, just wanting to get it over with.

Flint led her to Mac's truck where Mac greeted her kindly as she got into the passenger seat. Once she was settled in, the caravan left the clearing and headed toward town.

"I can't thank you all enough for doing this for me," she said to Mac.

He flashed her a quick smile. "From what Flint told us, you're doing the right thing and we don't mind helping out at all to get a pervert off the streets."

"Still, I really appreciate it," she replied.

"No problem. At least we now know why Flint has been ditching us in the evenings and spending so much time at the cabin. He built that cabin as a place to get away from everyone and everything. It's nice to know he's been sharing it with you."

"I've been cooking dinner for him each evening," she replied. She found herself telling Mac about her arrangement with Flint. Talking about it was easier than thinking about talking to Chief Bowie about Brad.

She finally fell silent and stared out the passenger window. Nerves once again began to twist her stomach as they entered the edge of town.

There was no way to gauge what the consequences of her actions might be and that was what scared her so badly. When word got out would people shun her in the streets? Would somebody try to hurt her for speaking out about one of the town's favorite sons? What kind of repercussions would there be?

When Mac pulled up in front of the police station on Main Street, he told her to sit tight until all the other men were parked and getting out of their trucks.

Once they were out, only then did Mac tell her to get out of his truck. When she did the men all gathered around her like she was some sort of a rock star and they were her highly paid bodyguards.

Annie O'Brian, the police dispatcher, greeted

them all with raised brows as they filled the small receptionist area inside the police station.

"Uh, I'll go get Dillon." She jumped up from her desk and disappeared behind a closed door. When she returned, the tall, dark-haired chief of police was behind her.

"Gentlemen…and Maddy." He greeted them with obvious surprise. "What can I do for you all?"

"Madison needs to speak with you in private," Flint said.

"Maddy, follow me," Dillon said.

She turned to Flint and grabbed his hand. "Come with me?"

Flint nodded and together they followed Dillon to his private office. Dillon eased down in his chair behind his large wooden desk and gestured them to two straight-backed chairs that faced him. "So what's going on?"

Madison swallowed hard and squeezed Flint's hand tightly. "I… I'm here to report an assault."

Dillon pulled out a piece of paper and a pen. "What kind of an assault are you reporting?"

"I… I was beaten and raped." Her voice trembled uncontrollably and she swallowed hard in an effort to calm herself.

Dillon sat up straighter in his chair and his gray eyes flashed darkly. "Where did this occur?"

"At my trailer."

"And when did it happen?" Dillon asked.

And with that Madison told him everything. She shared with him every ugly detail of the attack and while she did she couldn't look at Flint. Even though he'd already heard what had happened, she didn't want to see any pity in his eyes.

She told Dillon not only about the first attack, but also that her rapist had come back and how she'd barred her door so he couldn't get in. She ended with the morning Flint had found her in the Holiday barn.

"And who did this to you, Maddy?" Dillon asked.

She hesitated a long moment. "Brad Ainsworth," she finally replied.

Thankfully, the lawman didn't raise an eyebrow or show any hint of skepticism. Instead, he began to ask her more questions about the attack.

"Are you going to arrest him?" she finally asked when it seemed like every question he could possibly ask had been answered.

"Maddy, it's not that easy, especially since this happened several months ago. First, I'm going to need to conduct an investigation," Dillon replied.

"So he won't be arrested today?" she asked with a simmering sense of panic.

"It's doubtful," Dillon replied.

"Madison has been staying in a cabin I have and she doesn't want anyone to know that's where she is," Flint said. "That's why all the men came with us this morning, so Brad won't know where she is and who is hiding her."

"I'm scared," Madison said softly to Dillon. "I know what Brad is capable of and he scares me half to death."

"There's no reason for him to know where you are," Dillon assured her. "These are serious allegations and I intend to take this matter very seriously. I will probably need to speak to you again at some point, but we'll make sure any further interviews take place wherever you're most comfortable."

Madison breathed a small sigh of relief. Hopefully, Brad would never know where she was staying and sooner rather than later he would be arrested. Before they finished up the interview, Dillon got directions to Flint's cabin and Flint told him the phone number of his landline.

Minutes later they walked out of the office where all the other cowboys were waiting. With Dillon's promise that he would call Flint when he had an update for them, they all left the building.

She rode back to the cabin with Jerod Steen. She'd always found him rather intimidating even though she knew in his spare time he worked with a lot of the youth in town at the community center.

They made some small talk and then she fell deep into her thoughts. She didn't know whether she felt better or worse by talking to Dillon. At the moment a veil of numbness had fallen over her. All she wanted was to get to the cabin and curl up in her bed beneath the covers.

When they reached the cabin the rest of the men left, but Flint stayed. After they walked through the door, to her surprise, Flint pulled her into his arms.

She leaned into his broad chest and reveled in the safety she felt in his embrace. He smelled of soap and sunshine with a hint of fresh cologne.

"I'm so proud of you," he said softly.

Her heart expanded and she raised her head to gaze at him. "Nobody has ever said those words to me before."

He looked at her in surprise. "Not even your father?"

She released a small, bitter laugh. "My father only spoke to me to tell me what he wanted for dinner. I spent eighteen years trying to win his approval, but never succeeded."

"I'm sorry, Madison. You deserved so much better than that." His eyes were so warm and his mouth was so close to hers. A heat rushed through her.

His gaze moved from her eyes to her lips and she leaned even closer into him. And then his mouth was on hers. It began as a gentle kiss, but when she parted her lips to him the kiss quickly became something hot and wild.

His tongue swirled with hers and sweet heat rushed over her. She leaned more intimately into him and released a small moan.

Suddenly, he pulled his lips from hers, dropped his arms from around her and took a step backward. "I'm so sorry," he said. "I… I shouldn't have done that."

Madison raised her fingers to her lips where the heat of his kiss still lingered. She dropped her arm back to her side. "I didn't mind it," she replied. "In fact, I liked it. I liked it a lot."

Flint's eyes flared wide and he took another step back from her. "You've already been violated by one man. I certainly don't want to be another man who takes advantage of you."

"Flint, you've treated me with the utmost respect since the moment you found me hiding in the barn. I wanted you to kiss me." She felt the warmth that leaped into her cheeks. "I've been wanting it."

He shoved his hands in his pockets and she heard the jingle of his keys. "We probably shouldn't kiss again," he replied, his gaze not quite meeting hers.

"Why not?" she asked.

"It's just probably not a good idea. Now, how about we eat some lunch?" He headed toward the refrigerator.

She wanted to ask him why it wasn't a good idea for them to kiss. He'd stirred her like nothing else she'd experienced in her entire life. But it was obvious he was uncomfortable with any more discussion on the matter.

"Go sit at the table and I'll get lunch," she told

him. She needed to do something to take her mind off how much she'd loved being in Flint's arms and having his lips on hers. And if she wasn't thinking about that she'd be worrying about Brad and what was going to happen when he learned she'd gone to the police about his beating and rape of her.

She fixed them sandwiches and thankfully, their conversation revolved around nothing important. "Don't you have to go back to work at the ranch this afternoon?" she asked when they were finished eating.

"Not if you need for me to hang around here," he replied.

Oh, she wanted him to hang around here. There was a simmering fear deep inside her now that she'd spoken to the police. She didn't want to be all alone here, but she also knew Flint had gone above and beyond for her already and she couldn't ask anything more from him. She had to be strong.

"I love your company, but you need to get back to work. You have done everything in your power to make sure I stay safe here and I'm sure I'll be fine. I'll just see you for dinner."

"Are you sure you'll be okay?" His gaze searched her features.

She forced a bright smile. "Definitely. Now, go on, get out of here and make sure you thank all the men who helped us this morning." She walked with him to the door.

"Then I guess I'll see you for dinner, but if anything happens…if you get scared for any reason, you call me and I'll be right back here."

"Thanks, Flint…for everything."

He smiled, that sexy slide of lips that made her want to lean into him and kiss him all over again. "I'm really proud of you, Madison. You're a beautiful, strong woman and I'm glad I found you hiding out in the barn." With those words he turned around and headed toward his truck.

She closed and locked the door behind him as a wealth of emotion pressed tight against her chest. She would soon be four months pregnant with her rapist's baby and she was precariously close to falling in love with a handsome, strong cowboy named Flint McCay. It would be so easy to envision him as her forever cowboy.

Mac had told her that Flint had built this place as somewhere to get away from everything and everyone. She knew he had built it for a time when he'd stop working on the Holiday Ranch. But she could see herself here with him, not just temporarily, but forever.

Two weeks before she'd run from her trailer, she had finally gotten up the nerve to venture out of her home. She'd gone to the library and had begun reading some self-help books on rape and victimization.

As she'd sat at one of the computers late one af-

ternoon, she'd begun to weep. One of the young li-
brarians, Amy Leyton, had come over to the desk
to check on her.

Amy instantly noticed what book she was reading and without prying, she had offered not only a
comforting hug, but also a recommendation of an
online support group.

Madison had instantly joined the group and for
the next two days she had spent hours not only
"talking" to other victims, but also claiming back
some of her sense of self.

She still had a long way to go toward complete
healing, but when this was over she would see a
therapist to help her heal even more.

She was scared of Brad Ainsworth, but she was
also afraid that she was such damaged goods that
no good man would ever want her.

Flint might be kind to her, he even might be
sexually attracted to her, but she had a feeling she
would never be his forever kind of woman and right
now…at this very moment…that made her incredibly sad.

All Flint could think about as he worked throughout the afternoon was kissing Madison. Her lips had
been so soft and inviting. He'd not only wanted to
continue kissing her, but he'd also wanted to take
her into his bedroom and make slow, sweet love to
her and that desire stunned him.

I've been wanting it. Her words played and replayed through his mind. She'd shocked him when she'd said that. She'd shocked him and created a roaring fire inside him at the same time.

He should be ashamed of himself for even entertaining such heated thoughts about her, but that didn't stop him from thinking about it. She was so charming, so beautiful, and it was only natural that he would be attracted to her.

He was the wrong man for her. She wanted a cowboy as her forever man, and once her issues here were settled and she moved from his cabin, he would quit his job here at the ranch and he wouldn't be a cowboy anymore.

Besides, at the moment she was all alone in the world. She was grateful to Flint for taking her in, for being kind to her. It was probably that gratefulness that had made her want to kiss him.

Hopefully, Brad Ainsworth would be arrested soon and when that happened Madison would be free to go back to her trailer and resume her normal life. It would be nice if when that happened they could part ways as good friends.

She was the first woman he'd ever known who he felt comfortable around. He'd never been able to talk so easily to a woman as he was able to talk to Madison.

His emotions where she was concerned were so

confusing. He liked her a lot, but she also stirred a rich desire in him that he'd never felt before.

She had been violently violated by Brad, and Flint would shoot himself if he thought that anything he did somehow violated her even more. That was the very last thing he'd ever want to do.

"Hey, Flint."

Flint looked up from the harness he'd been oiling to see Sawyer Quincy. "Hi, Sawyer."

Sawyer was the ranch foreman and one of the men Flint considered his brother. The sandy-haired man had recently married Janis Little, a woman who worked as a waitress at the Watering Hole. He'd moved off the ranch and now lived with Janis in a house they'd bought in town. He was also one of the cowboys who had gone into the police station that morning with Madison.

"How is Maddy doing after this afternoon?" Sawyer asked.

"She's okay, although scared now that she's gone to the police." Flint frowned as a rich rage filled his head. "I'd love to get hold of Brad and beat the living hell out of him. But I know once I started hitting him, I wouldn't be able to stop until he was near death."

"And then you'd be in jail and Madison would be all on her own," Sawyer replied.

"That's the only reason I won't go after him," Flint replied darkly.

Sawyer shook his head. "I can't believe Brad Ainsworth is such a sick son of a bitch. He's been like the golden boy in town with all his charity work and good deeds."

"It's not the first time we've all been fooled by an evil man," Flint replied as his heart constricted with a sense of betrayal.

"You're talking about Adam," Sawyer said.

Flint nodded. Adam Benson had been one of the men Flint and the others had grown up with, a man they had considered their brother until it was revealed that he was a serial killer with a sick soul.

All the men had been stunned when it was learned that he'd killed half a dozen boys when they'd been young. He'd killed them and then buried them on the property. It was only when work was started on a new shed that the skeletal remains had been revealed.

The police investigation had been stymied until as an adult Adam had gone after Cassie with an ax. Thankfully, Dillon had gotten to her in time to save her life and she and Dillon had been together ever since.

None of the other "boys" had seen the killer in Adam. None of them had even seen a glimpse of the evil inside him. When his crimes had finally come to light, it had felt like such a deep betrayal.

"I guess you never know if there's evil in a man's heart unless he somehow shows it," Sawyer said.

"Brad showed his to a vulnerable woman who trusted him for a simple ride home on a rainy night." Flint's hands clenched into fists at his sides as the rage reared its head inside him once again.

"You have to trust that Dillon will get this right, Flint," Sawyer said. "Meanwhile, how are you doing? I've occasionally heard you groan a bit as you get up from the table at breakfast."

A wave of embarrassment swept through Flint but he forced what he hoped was an easy smile. "Oh, you know…all those years of bull-riding are starting to catch up with me. I've got a little arthritis in my hip."

Sawyer grinned. "I think we're all starting to feel the foolishness of our youth. My shoulder still hurts on rainy days since I tried to arm-wrestle with Jerod two years ago."

Flint laughed. "As I recall, you challenged him about fifteen times looking for a win."

"And fifteen times he put me down," Sawyer said with a hearty laugh. He clapped Flint on the back and then looked at his watch. "I just wanted to check in with you and it's late enough in the day that if you just want to knock off, then I'll see you in the morning."

As soon as Sawyer left the stable, Flint began to put his work tools away. When he was finished, he walked outside and noticed Dillon's patrol car was parked in front of the house. He was either home for dinner or was taking a break.

Instead of heading to the vehicle shed to get his truck, he walked to the large, white, two-story house that Cassie and Dillon called home. He wanted to check in with Dillon before he went to the cabin to spend the evening with Madison.

Cassie answered the knock on the back door. She was a pretty, petite blonde who ran the ranch with an iron fist, just like big Cass, who had left the place to her.

"Flint." She smiled warmly and opened the door wider. "Come on in."

He walked into the kitchen where Dillon was seated at the table with a cup of coffee before him. "Hi, Flint. I just stopped by to see my wife before hitting the road again." He gestured toward the chair opposite him.

"Coffee?" Cassie asked him.

"No, thanks. I'm good." He sat across from Dillon. "I was just wondering if you'd had a chance to interview Brad and if there was anything I could take back to Madison."

"I did speak with Brad and he immediately denied the charges."

"Of course he did," Flint said with disgust. "Did he mention having any idea why Madison would file these 'false' charges against him?"

"Actually, he did. He said that he knew Maddy

had a big crush on him and when she asked him to have dinner with her, he turned her down and told her he had no interest in her. He said she's obviously made up this story to get back at him."

"What a load of horse crap," Flint replied. "So what happens now?"

"Right now it's a he said-she said situation. I'll be talking to any woman Brad has dated in the past to see what their experiences were with him. I'll also be talking to his friends to see if I can gain any information that will move the investigation forward," Dillon said. "I'm also checking with everyone at the trailer park to see if anyone saw Brad on either night that Maddy said he was there."

Dillon paused and took a drink from his coffee cup. He set the cup back down and frowned at Flint. "I've got to tell you, this case would have been so much easier if Maddy had come forward immediately when it happened. Then we would have had DNA evidence and since she said that Brad beat her there would have been evidence of that, as well. With that we could have built a strong case. It's problematic that this happened over three months ago."

"But unfortunately that didn't happen. She didn't report it at the time. She was too frightened to come forward." Flint sighed. It sounded like this was all going to take some time before Brad would be behind bars. Certainly more time than Madison had thought.

"As long as Madison is safely hidden away at my cabin, we'll get through this, and I have to believe that justice will be served."

"As chief of police, that's always my goal," Dillon replied. "Trust me, Flint. I'm taking this case very seriously. I'm going to speak with the DA and see if he will proceed to take the case right now and then I can get Brad under arrest."

"That would definitely make Madison rest easier."

"And please tell Maddy she's in my thoughts and prayers," Cassie added.

"Thanks, I will." Flint stood. "I won't take up any more of your time."

Dillon got up from the table, too. "I'll be in touch with you if I learn anything more."

Minutes later Flint was on his way back to the cabin. Madison wasn't going to be happy when he told her Brad's side of the story, but she needed to know what he'd said. Hopefully, the DA would agree to move the case forward.

On another note, it also bothered him that apparently he'd been moaning and groaning enough with his pain that Sawyer had taken notice. Maybe it was time for him to check out that prescription the doctor had written out for him.

He shoved this thought out of his mind. Right

now he had to focus on Madison and her needs. He wanted her to feel safe. He wanted to keep her safe. However, as he drew closer to the cabin and a desire began to simmer in the pit of his stomach, he wondered if right now the man he needed to protect her from was himself.

Brad sat on the sofa in his perfectly decorated apartment. He was proud of his personal space, just as he was proud of the life he'd been building in Bitterroot.

In his day-to-day life he worked as a successful insurance salesman, but his ultimate goal was to step into his father's shoes as mayor of the small town.

Of course, that would be just the beginning of what he saw for himself in politics. He wanted an illustrious career, one that would ultimately take him out of this dusty, boring town and to the good life in Washington DC. He was young, good-looking and smart. He had all the qualities and plans to make his dreams come true.

And that bitch wanted to ruin it all for him.

He clenched his fists so tightly his fingernails bit into the palms of his hands. Maddy Taylor…what was he going to do about Maddy Taylor?

None of the other women had come forward. None of them had dared to tell the law about his dark desire. So why had she?

Brad knew he was a monster. He knew it wasn't normal to take pleasure in the sight of a woman bloodied by his fists and sobbing for him to stop. But he was hardwired that way. He got the most intense sexual pleasure while taking a woman against her will.

He'd always tried to drive into Oklahoma City and use a prostitute for his twisted pleasures. However, there had been times when he had taken his pleasure right here in his own hometown.

He'd been so careful. He'd only shown that side of himself to a couple of women here in Bitterroot who were way below his social standing, women who were timid and shy and rarely had a voice.

But that bitch Maddy had found her voice and had shot it off to Dillon. He'd heard from a couple of his friends that she'd shown up at the police station with a bunch of dumb cowboys from the Holiday Ranch.

He stood and instantly plumped and rearranged the throw pillows on the sofa. His friends teased him about being a bit on the OCD side. He liked a clean place. He liked everything to be in its place. And now Maddy Taylor needed to be put in her place.

Since he saw her car on the side of the road, he'd been unable to locate her. But now he had a clue. One of the Holiday cowboys was obviously helping her…hiding her.

All he had to do was figure out who it was and then he would be able to put Maddy in her place... in a shallow grave.

Chapter 7

Madison opened the door to Flint, her heart expanding at the very sight of him. Being alone in the cabin after telling Dillon about Brad had been unsettling. She had jumped at every noise and had looked outside the windows a hundred times.

But she'd gotten through it by focusing on the kiss, that wonderful, soul-stirring kiss that she and Flint had shared. It had fired a hot desire through her that she'd never felt before.

She now smiled at him as he approached her. "Hey, cowboy, it's good to see you again."

He grinned, that sexy smile of his that made a rush of heat sweep through her. "Hmm, as usual something smells good in here," he said as he walked into the cabin.

"That would be dinner," she replied.

He took off his hat and tossed it to the sofa. "Can I do anything to help?"

"Nope. Just sit."

He sank down in his chair at the table. "How was your afternoon?" he asked.

She pulled the smothered steak out of the oven and then turned to look at him. "To be honest, I was a little nervous being here all alone. I just hope Brad never finds out I'm here."

"There's no reason to believe he'll find this place. None of the men who were with us this morning will breathe a word to anyone else about this cabin."

His words comforted her. If he believed in his cowboy buddies that much, then she would believe in them, as well. She busied herself getting the meal served and then joined him at the table to eat. "So how was your afternoon?" she asked.

She loved to listen to him talk about his work on the ranch and his interaction with the other men. While she was grateful to be here in the cabin, she missed having daily interactions with other people.

She wanted to be safe, but she looked forward to the time when this thing with Brad was behind her and she could go back to her job at the grocery store. She desperately wanted to somehow reclaim some of the good pieces of her former life.

"Did you hear anything more from Dillon?" she asked once the dishes were cleared away and the two of them had moved into the living room. He picked up his hat and tossed it into the nearby chair and they sat side by side.

Flint hesitated before answering her question and immediately a ball of tension knotted in her chest. "Flint?"

"Yeah, I talked to Dillon right before coming here."

"And?"

"And he'd already interviewed Brad," Flint replied.

"What did Brad tell him?" The ball of tension tightened inside her.

"That it didn't happen, that he would never do something like that to any woman. He said you only charged him with this because you were interested in him and he rejected you."

She stared at Flint for several long moments. She wanted to cry, but before she could fully embrace that emotion, a rich anger swept through her instead.

She jumped up off the sofa. "Damn him," she blurted. "Damn him to hell for what he did to me and now making up a story about me wanting any kind of a romantic relationship with him. God, that makes me want to puke."

"Madison, don't get yourself all worked up. It's not good for the baby." He took her by the hand and urged her to sit back down. "Dillon has only just started the investigation. You shouldn't be surprised that Brad denied the allegation."

Flint's words calmed her, not so much for herself, but for the baby she carried. He released her hand as she sat back down next to him. "Of course I didn't expect him to confess, but I can't believe he told Dillon that I made all this up for some sort of sick revenge because I had some sort of crush on him."

"I hope you don't regret coming forward." Flint picked up her hand once again. Calloused by work, his grip engulfed hers and made her feel safe.

And all of a sudden she was thinking of the kiss they had shared and wanting him to take her lips with his again. She not only wanted him to kiss her, she also wanted him to take her into his bedroom and make sweet love to her.

She had never felt as close to a man as she felt in this moment with Flint. She wanted him to fill her head with a memory of sweet lovemaking to replace the violent, pain-filled memory of Brad's rape. This would be on her terms. She would give to Flint what was hers to give and in the process claim yet another piece of herself back.

She leaned into him. "I don't regret taking this to Dillon. Somebody has to stop Brad from ever hurting another woman and as long as I know you're by my side, I'll be just fine."

"And I'll stay by your side until this is all over." His green eyes were warm, like the grass on a beautiful sunny day and she wanted to lie in them, lie in him.

She raised her face and parted her lips, hoping he would see her open invitation and take her mouth with his once again. Apparently, he didn't get what she wanted or was afraid to overstep his boundaries. He smiled at her and then glanced away.

"Flint." He looked at her once again.

"Flint, kiss me," she said softly.

His eyes flamed as if suddenly shot through with bright neon lights. "Madison, I told you earlier this afternoon that we shouldn't do any more of that."

His slightly husky voice let her know his words meant nothing, that despite what he said he wouldn't mind kissing her once again. "But why shouldn't we?" She moved a little closer to him, close enough that their thighs touched.

He smelled so good. It was the scent of sunshine and the fragrance of his cologne that had become as familiar to her as her own heartbeat. She wanted to wrap herself up in it and wear it against her naked skin. "Don't you want to kiss me again?"

He drew in an audible breath. "Oh, woman,

you're killing me here." His eyes flamed once again and he quickly looked away from her. "Of course I'd like to kiss you again, but you're vulnerable right now, Madison. All of this has you shaken up and you might not really know what you want."

"Well, that's a load of baloney," she scoffed. "Look at me, Flint." She waited until his gaze was once again on her. "I know exactly what I want. I want you to kiss me long and hard."

She knew by the glaze of his eyes and his sudden intake of breath that he was going to do it, and it was going to be amazing.

His mouth took hers in a kiss that seared her to her soul. His hands tangled first in her long hair and then slid down her back to her waist. He tugged her closer to him as she opened her mouth to invite him in.

Their tongues danced together in a fiery swirl that half stole her breath away. Her hands rose to his broad shoulders and she gripped them tightly as a deep want rushed through her.

She didn't want just any man...she wanted this man. Her desire for him had nothing to do with her gratefulness. It had nothing to do with his protecting her.

Sure, it was a fire that had been born in his kindness, but it had been stoked by the way he sometimes looked at her and by how gentle he was whenever they touched. Her desire for him had risen with each conversation they'd shared and with the tears she'd shed with him and as he had comforted her.

These were only fleeting thoughts as their kiss continued. He finally tore his mouth from hers and trailed his lips down her cheek and across her jawline. She moved her hands to his hair and her lips toward his left ear.

"Make love to me, Flint. Take me into your bedroom and make sweet love to me," she whispered.

He jerked back from her, his quickened breaths sounding loudly in the otherwise silent room. Or was it her own breaths she heard? His eyes were even more glazed than they had been before. "Madison, we can't." The huskiness in his voice told her that he wanted her as much as she did him.

"Yes, we can. I want you, and I know you want me, so why shouldn't we?" She stood and held out her hand to him. "Please, Flint. I want you so badly."

He got to his feet and once again she was in his arms and his mouth covered hers in a fiery kiss that spoke of his desire for her. When the kiss ended, without a word they went into his bedroom.

"Are you sure, Madison?" he asked. "I need to know you're very sure about this."

"I've never been more certain about anything in my life. I want you, Flint."

He pulled her close and kissed her once again.

They kissed on for what felt like forever, but it was as if he was afraid to touch her anyplace else. And she wanted more…oh so much more from him.

"Flint, unzip my dress," she whispered as she pulled her lips from his.

His hands went to the back zipper of the long, floral summer dress she wore. She felt the hesitation in him, but she leaned into him to encourage him. The zipper whispered down and he pushed the dress off her shoulders. It pooled into a bed of flowers at her feet and left her clad only in her bra and panties.

"Oh, God, Madison, you are absolutely gorgeous." His gaze swept the length of her, as hot as a physical touch.

She placed her hands over the growing bump of her tummy. He reached out and pulled her hands away. "Don't hide that. It's new life and it's beautiful."

She nearly melted. If she hadn't wanted him before this moment, his words would have had her running for his naked arms. She moved in front of him and grabbed the bottom of his T-shirt and yanked it up. He aided her by taking it off the rest of the way and tossing it to the chair in the corner of the room.

He then walked to the bed and pulled down the black-and-gray bedspread, exposing white sheets. She immediately got into the bed and watched as he took off his boots and his socks. He then unbuttoned his fly, unzipped his jeans and took them off.

He was beautiful with his broad shoulders and his six-pack of muscles. His stomach was flat, his hips were slim and he was already aroused.

He got into bed and pulled her into an embrace that had them touching from chest to toes. Her skin loved the feel of his, all his warm flesh overlaying firm muscle. Their lips locked again in a sizzling kiss and she was lost in him.

He changed positions, freeing one of his arms so he could caress her. His hand moved slowly from her neck, across her collarbones and to one of her breasts.

She could feel the heat of his palm through the wispy bra material. But she wanted to be completely naked in his arms. She raised up and reached behind her to unfasten the bra hooks. He plucked the garment away from her and threw it to the floor next to the bed.

She wiggled out of her panties and he took off his boxers. He embraced her again, and this time there were no clothing barriers between them.

He moved to touch her breasts again. The sensation of his work-roughened hand evoked a moan from her. Then his fingers found her taut nipple and sizzling electric currents rushed through her. When his mouth followed his fingers and he licked, sweet, hot desire overtook her and she moaned again.

He raised his head and looked at her. Desire lit his eyes, but there was something else there…a softness in the green glow of his gaze that almost shattered her. After what had happened to her, she needed his softness, his gentleness.

"If I move too fast or make you uncomfortable in any way, tell me," he said.

"I will, but you're doing just fine." To prove that to him she reached down and wrapped her hand around the length of his hardness.

He moaned and his hand moved down to the very center of her. She was already moist and ready for him. His fingers played against her, and her pleasure spiraled upward.

"Yes, yes," she said, her breaths becoming pants. In return she pumped her hand up and down him. She arched her hips upward to meet his fingers and then she was there, falling over a precipice as she cried out his name.

"Flint, I need you now," she said with a gasp. She released her hold on him and instead urged him to move between her parted thighs.

He hovered over her with hesitation. She gripped him by the buttocks and urged him forward. He entered her slowly and she closed her eyes as tears of joy rose up inside her.

He wasn't taking from her, she was willingly giving herself to him. And no matter what happened in the future, she would have Flint's sweet lovemaking to remember instead of memories of this being taken from her against her will.

She arched up to meet his strokes and once again she climbed upward with a wild desire she had never felt before. She clung to him, her hands gripping his broad shoulders.

And then she was there again, riding a wave of exquisite pleasure. At the same time Flint stiffened against her, reaching his own orgasm.

They remained locked together for several long minutes and then he kissed her, a tender kiss that spoke of a caring she'd never felt from any man.

After the kiss he rolled away from her and smiled. "I'll let you use the bathroom first."

"Thank you." She got out of the bed and padded to the bathroom naked. She felt no need to cover herself, but she did feel the heat of his gaze on her as she walked.

Once there, she stared at herself in the mirror. Her cheeks were flushed with color and in this moment she was happier than she'd ever been in her entire life. The only thing that could make it better was if she got to fall asleep in his arms.

She left the bathroom and he passed her to go in. She knew when he came back into the room he'd probably get dressed to head back to the ranch.

She found her panties next to the bed, pulled

them back on and then slid back beneath the sheets. She was hoping to change his mind about leaving. He opened the bathroom door and hesitated in the threshold when he saw her in the bed.

"Can you stay here with me tonight, Flint?" she asked. "Just this one night can I sleep here in your arms?"

He didn't say a word. He walked over and grabbed his black boxers from the floor. He pulled them on and then slid into the bed next to her. They faced each other and in his gaze she saw a bit of regret.

"Madison…" he began.

She raised a finger to his lips. "Please, don't talk…just cuddle." She turned to the other side and then moved her backside into him, spoon style.

He wrapped an arm around her and pulled her closer against him. She didn't want him to say anything to ruin what had happened between them. She didn't want to hear any regrets he might have.

She definitely had no regrets. She cared deeply about Flint, and making love with him had been a gift she'd given to herself…and it had been a wonderful, magical gift.

He might not realize it but he had given her an amazing gift, as well. He'd made her remember gentleness and respect while making love. He'd made her remember that there were good and kind men who didn't take what a woman didn't offer.

With the warmth of his body next to hers and with his arm wrapped across her tummy, she fell into sweet dreams.

Flint's first vestiges of awakeness came with the sweet, floral scent of Madison eddying in his head. That was followed by the feel of her warmth and the curves of her body in his arms.

Even though he was awake, he remained for several long minutes with his eyes closed and relished the simple joy of being so close to her. He loved the scent of her and how neatly she fit against him.

He finally opened his eyes. The room was still dark, but he knew within the next thirty minutes or so the first peek of the sun would appear in the eastern skies.

It was time for him to get out of bed. He needed to get up before he became aroused from her nearness. He also needed to head back to the ranch, but there was no question he was reluctant to leave his bed. Madison slept peacefully and even though he would rather stay here with her than leave, he knew he needed to get up and go.

He couldn't think with her nestled in his arms and he definitely needed to think after what had happened between them. In fact, as wonderful as it had been, he now wished it had never happened. The last thing she needed to believe was that he was going to be somebody special in her life, that he was going to be the cowboy of her dreams.

As if he needed a reminder of this, his joints screamed out when he untangled himself from her and slid out of the bed. Thankfully, she didn't wake up as he dressed and then left the cabin.

During the drive he thought about what they had done. There was no question he'd loved making love to her. She'd been warm and giving and exciting, everything he'd want in a lover.

But he didn't want her to entertain any false illusions about the two of them. She had no future with him. Eventually, she would meet the cowboy who would be right for her, one who could give her the dream life she wanted. But that cowboy wasn't him and could never be him.

She needed his protection right now, and he needed to support her in her quest for justice where Brad was concerned. But once that issue was addressed she would be able to go back to life in her trailer where she would be ready to meet the cowboy of her dreams.

When he reached the ranch, he parked and then went directly to his room. He took a long, hot shower, not only to wash away the scent of Madison that might cling to him, but also to ease some of the aches and pains in his body.

When he was dressed for the day, he headed to the dining room for breakfast. It was early enough that Cookie hadn't yet put out the food, but the large silver coffeepot was ready to serve, and Mac and Jerod were already at one of the tables with cups of the hot brew in hand.

Flint greeted them and then got himself a cup of coffee and joined them at the table. "What's up, gentlemen?" he asked.

"Nothing much with us, but Maddy is definitely the talk of the town," Mac said.

Flint winced. "So word is out about her allegations against Brad?"

"Oh yeah, definitely. I went into town for some supplies at the feed store yesterday and Mr. Tanner asked me if I knew anything about it," Jerod said.

"What did you tell him?" Flint asked.

"That if he wanted to know anything about it, then he should ask Chief Bowie."

"And I was at the diner last night where it seemed like everyone in the place was talking about it," Mac said.

"What were they saying?" Flint asked, although he wasn't sure he really wanted to know.

"It was just a lot of speculation about whether the allegations were true or not. But I've got to tell you, it sounded like most people were coming down firmly on Brad's side, especially the men."

Flint frowned. "That's what I was afraid of."

"You've got to remember that Brad has spent

years building up his reputation as an intelligent, generous and all-round stellar person," Mac said.

"It makes me sick to think of what he did to Madison," Flint replied. "Did either of you see the man of the hour around?"

"No, but I think he might have followed me home from the diner," Mac replied.

"Really?" Flint straightened on the bench and took a sip of his coffee. There was only one reason Brad might have been following Mac home…and that was because Brad was attempting to find out which one of them was harboring Madison.

"Even if he eventually finds out where Madison is staying, he'd be a damn fool to do something to try to hurt her. He'd be the first suspect if anything happened to her," Mac said.

"He might be a complete monster in the dark, but he isn't a stupid man," Jerod added. "Right now it's just a case of he said-she said. But if he threatens Maddy in any way or if he does anything to her, then it definitely tips the scales in Maddy's favor."

Everything they said continued to whirl around in Flint's head while he ate breakfast and then got to work for the day. Was Brad really stupid enough to try to hurt Madison? Would he be desperate enough to try to shut her up forever?

He'd understood Madison's desire to keep her location a secret. He also knew why she didn't want to go back to her trailer where she might be vulnerable to him attacking her again. But he hadn't really thought about her being in any real physical danger, not with Dillon knowing the facts of the case.

By the time everyone knocked off at noon for lunch, instead of going to the rec room to eat, Flint headed to the big house to talk with Cassie.

He'd mentally considered all the options. His brain was half-exhausted, and on top of that physically it had been a tough pain day.

Cassie answered the door on the first knock and ushered him into the kitchen where the two of them sat at the table. "I wanted to ask you if I could take some vacation time," he said.

She raised a blond eyebrow. "Maddy?"

He nodded. "She's really afraid right now and I want to be there for her until everything is resolved one way or another. She's been through a lot."

"You know you have lots of vacation time coming to you, so there's no problem there. I want you to do what you need to do for that poor woman."

"So you believe her?" Flint asked.

"I know Maddy and she would never make up a story like that." Cassie's blue eyes darkened. "I never liked that smooth-talking, glad-handing Brad. I always felt like something was off with him."

"I only hope Dillon finds some evidence that supports Madison. And thanks for giving me time off." He rose from the table.

"I'm not giving you anything," she said with a

smile. "You've earned what you're taking." She walked him to the door. "Go ahead and take off now. Just tell Sawyer what's going on so he can take you off the chores list."

"Thanks, Cassie." They said their goodbyes and as he walked away from the house he knew that sooner rather than later he was going to have to tell Cassie that he was quitting his job for good as one of her cowboys.

A wave of depression swept over him. If not a cowboy, then what would he be? His whole identity was tied to being a cowboy. When he stopped that, then who would he become?

He shoved these thoughts away. He couldn't think about his own future right now. All he wanted to focus on was assuring that Madison had a bright and happy future and he'd figure out his own later.

At least he could tell her that Cassie believed her claims. That would go a long way in making Madison think she'd done the right thing in coming forward.

He went around to the lunchroom and looked for Sawyer. He spied him sitting at a table across the room, laughing with several of the other men.

"Sawyer, can I speak to you for a minute?"

"Sure." Sawyer immediately got up from the table and stepped away from the other men and then gave Flint his sole attention. "What's up?" he asked.

Flint explained to him about taking some time off and that he was leaving the ranch immediately. Sawyer assured him it was no problem and within minutes Flint was in his room and packing two large duffel bags.

Unfortunately, the first thing he needed to do was have a serious talk with Madison. He needed to make sure she understood that what happened last night between them could never happen again.

It was as much for his own good as for hers. Last night had brought out feelings in him that he'd never felt before for any woman. It was already going to be difficult for him to say goodbye to her. If they shared more of that kind of intimacy it would only make it all even more difficult.

He also didn't want her spinning any fantasies where he was concerned. Yes, he'd given her a place to live, and yes, he had and would continue to support her through the darkness of this thing that was Brad, but he wasn't, and could never be, anything permanent in her life.

Finished with his packing, he then threw the duffel bags into the back of his pickup and headed for the cabin. There was no question he was dreading the talk he was going to have with Madison, but he had to make sure that they were both on the same page, especially since he intended to now be at the cabin full-time.

She deserved far better than a broke-down man

who didn't even know who he would be or what he might do in the future. He had to make it clear to her that eventually they would be going their own separate ways.

Chapter 8

It had been wonderful waking up in Flint's bed with the scent of him remaining in the sheets. Madison had lingered there after waking, reliving each and every moment of their lovemaking. It had been wonderful…magical even. It would be nice to have the memory of a man's hands touching her gently… tenderly, instead of the brutality of Brad's attack.

Even though she and Flint had been together intimately last night, already she wanted to repeat it. She wanted to explore his body all over again. She couldn't wait to make love with him again.

She finally got out of bed and showered and dressed in one of her summer dresses. It was a good thing when she'd believed she'd be leaving Bitterroot, she'd shoved as many clothes as possible into her suitcase. Her baby bump was definitely showing now, and she was grateful that the morning sickness issue apparently was long gone.

Once dressed, she wandered the living room restlessly. She was getting a bad case of cabin fever. She missed seeing people and talking to them. She loved her evenings with Flint, but she missed going to the café, and being in the grocery store. She missed walking the streets of the small town and stopping to chat with people she knew and liked.

Sustaining the level of fear she felt toward Brad was utterly exhausting. There was no way she could endure it for any real length of time. And she didn't want to stay in this cabin without seeing other people for days or weeks to come.

She'd already spent far too long holed up in her trailer, afraid to venture out except for her trips to the library, for fear of running into Brad. At least the library had been less than a block away from the trailer park and definitely not Brad's stomping grounds…at least during the daytime.

It was just after noon when she heard a truck approaching. She ran to the front window and breathed a sigh of relief as she saw Flint's vehicle.

What was he doing here so early? He never came here during work hours. Delighted to see him, she opened the door to greet him. "Hey, cowboy, what are you doing back here so early in the day?"

"I decided to knock off early today," he replied. He grabbed a couple of bags out of the bed of his truck.

"What are you doing? Moving in?" she asked as he dropped the bags inside the door.

"Something like that."

Her stomach suddenly dropped as she looked at him worriedly. "Has something bad happened?"

"No, nothing like that," he assured her. "I've just decided to take a little time off from the ranch."

"Are you sure nothing bad has happened?"

"I'm positive."

"Then why are you moving in here?" She couldn't help the simmering alarm that sizzled through her veins.

"Madison, there is nothing wrong. I just decided to take a few weeks off and stay here full-time. To be honest, I wanted a break from the ranch."

She decided she had to believe him. Surely he would tell her if something had happened concerning Brad. "You want a cup of coffee?" she asked and moved to the counter with the pod machine.

"Sure, that sounds good." He slowly eased down at the table and she didn't miss the slight wince that crossed his features.

"Are you having some sort of pain, Flint?"

He hesitated and then nodded his head. "Old broken bones are talking to me a little bit lately."

"What do you do for it? Do you take pain pills?"

"Nah, nothing like that. I usually don't do much of anything."

She put the pod to work in the coffee machine and then turned back to face him. "Is it your back? I could give you a massage if you think it might help."

"No, it will be fine, but we do need to talk."

He looked so serious and her heart dipped into the pit of her stomach. It didn't take a rocket scientist to figure out what he might want to talk about. She had tried to shush him the night before, but she could tell by the firm look on his face that she wasn't going to be able to shush him right now.

They were silent until she placed his coffee cup in front of him and sat opposite him. "Please don't tell me you regret what happened last night," she said before he had a chance to say anything.

He frowned and stared down into his cup for a long moment.

When he finally looked up at her, her heart settled back where it belonged. She wasn't exactly sure what she read in those beautiful green eyes of his, but remorse didn't seem to be there.

"How can I regret what happened between us? It was awesome and you were amazing, but Madison, it really can't happen again."

Her heart swelled. At least he thought she was amazing. But his words both soothed her and confused her at the same time. "Why can't it happen again?"

He released a deep sigh and wrapped his big hands around his coffee cup. "Because it would be like repeating false promises to each other each time we'd make love. I intend to live the rest of my life alone, and once you get through your issues, you'll go back to living your own best life without me in it."

Her heart once again dipped downward. His words sounded so stark, so final. Even though she'd known that eventually...hopefully, she would probably be able to return to her trailer and resume normal life; she hadn't really thought about what the future would look like without Flint being in it. It was true; after last night she'd hoped he'd be in her future for a very long time.

She wanted to make love with him again and again, and she definitely didn't want to think about her future without him. She somehow hoped...her brain froze in confusion. She didn't know what she really hoped for in the future. But she had to assure him that last night hadn't been a mistake and if they wound up in bed together again it wouldn't be another mistake.

"Flint, I didn't take last night as any kind of a promise of anything. I'm not some silly teenage girl who had sex with a boy for the first time and now believes we're going to be together forever."

He offered her a small smile. "I can't imagine you ever being a silly teenage girl."

"I didn't have time to be silly when I was a teenager," she replied, grateful to see his smile. "On another note, I've been doing a lot of thinking this morning. I've been hiding out here because of my fear of Brad, but I'm kind of tired of hiding out."

He raised an eyebrow as she continued. "I would still like to keep the fact that I'm staying here a secret, but I have to confess I'm going a little stir-crazy."

"I'm not even sure what that means." A wrinkle of confusion danced across his forehead.

She worked up the courage she'd been grappling to claim all morning and drew a deep breath. "It means I'd like to go into town and have dinner at the café this evening."

He looked at her in obvious surprise. "Really?"

She hesitated a moment and then nodded firmly. "Really. People are probably talking about it and I want them to know I'm not ashamed. I want to walk into the café with my head held high."

"According to Mac and Jerod, people *are* starting to talk about it," Flint admitted.

Her blue eyes blazed. "Brad stole something from me, but I've decided he's not going to steal my ability to go out to dinner or to see other people or anything else from me. He's taken enough."

Flint's gaze warmed as it lingered on her. "Madison, your strength utterly amazes me."

She released an unsteady laugh. "Don't praise me too much. I'm still scared to death of Brad. I know more than anyone what he's capable of." A shiver threatened to work up her spine as she remembered the way his fists had pummeled her before he took his sick pleasure.

"When I spoke to Cassie earlier she told me that she believed your accusations against Brad."

A flutter of relief swept through her. "So maybe there will be other people in town who also believe me. I hope not everyone has turned against me over this."

"I'm sure there will be plenty of people on your side," he replied and then frowned once again. "If you're serious about going this evening, then I can arrange for a couple of the cowboys to meet us at the café so Brad doesn't know specifically that you're with me. I'm sure Mac and Jerod would be up for a meal out."

It was her turn to frown. "I don't want you to have to put somebody else out for me."

"Trust me. It will be fine. At least for this first time with you getting out of the house I'll make sure we have some of my friends with us. Just let me get unpacked and then I'll make a few phone calls."

Madison remained seated at the table as Flint disappeared into his bedroom. There was no question the idea of going into town scared the hell out of her. But everything she'd told Flint was the truth.

It was time for her to claim back some of her freedom. She didn't want Brad to take anything else from her and hiding out here day after day felt like a win for him.

She finally got up from the table, washed out Flint's cup and then moved to the sofa to wait for him to come out of his room.

She didn't want to dwell on the things he'd said to her about their lovemaking and their futures. If she thought about it too much she'd become depressed. Besides, nobody knew what the future held. All they had was the present, and in the present, in this moment, she was falling head over heels in love with a cowboy named Flint.

At five-thirty that evening Flint led Madison to his truck in the driveway. "Beautiful evening," he said once they were in the truck.

"Yes, it is," she agreed. "It doesn't feel quite as hot as it has been."

"Won't be long until fall will be here."

"That's my favorite time of year."

She started babbling about the smell of apples

and sitting in front of a warm fire. As she continued talking about the yearly fall celebration in town Flint realized much of her chatter came from nerves.

She finally fell silent as he turned into the Holiday Ranch driveway where Mac and Jerod waited for them. He turned to Madison. "Changed your mind yet?"

"No." She raised her chin a notch. "Although I hate that you had to involve your friends."

"Trust me. It's no bother for them. They're always up for dinner at the café."

The two men got into the backseat of the king-cab and the four of them were on their way. As Mac and Jerod talked with Madison about the weather and things on the ranch, Flint shot surreptitious looks at her.

She looked prettier than he'd ever seen her. The lightweight royal blue sweater she wore over a blue-flowered dress matched perfectly the color of her eyes and made her dark hair look rich and shiny. The sweater also hid the slight bulge of her belly, which he knew had been her goal. Although sooner or later people were going to know she was pregnant.

He found a parking space in front of the café and the four of them got out. Flint fought against a natural instinct to wrap his arm around Madison's shoulder and pull her close to him as they walked into the café.

On this first trip out he didn't want anyone to be able to identify that Madison was specifically with him, although he knew eventually the word would get out. Hopefully, even if somebody did realize Flint was the one helping her, the location of his cabin would remain a secret.

The minute they all walked in, an unnatural silence fell among the diners. Flint shot a glance at Madison, who raised her stubborn chin and led the way to a booth for the four of them.

The quiet only lasted for a couple of seconds and then the buzz of whispers filled the air. There was no question that Madison was the subject of furtive glances and gossip.

Carlee, a young woman who had served them a hundred times before, greeted them all with a smile. "Hey, Maddy, it's nice to see you," she added.

"Thanks, Carlee," Madison replied warmly. Flint knew she was pleased with Carlee's friendly greeting.

"As you probably know the special tonight is chicken-fried steak with mashed potatoes and sweet corn," Carlee told them.

"Ah, the all-carb choice," Madison replied. "I'll take that."

The others agreed to the same thing and Carlee

left with their orders. "How are you doing?" Flint asked Madison.

"I know people are talking and staring, but I'm doing okay." She smiled. With the warmth of that gesture and her sweet scent eddying around in his head, Flint was momentarily tongue-tied.

Thankfully, Mac started in, talking about the various offerings on the menu and then he and Jerod began to argue about what made the best burger.

"Bacon," Jerod said. "The best burger has bacon on it."

"Nah, it's got to have sweet onions on it," Mac replied.

Flint absently listened to them, his thoughts consumed with Madison. She was getting deep under his skin. Flint had never dreamed there would be a woman like Madison, a woman he felt so comfortable with, one he wanted to spend time with and continue to get to know. He'd never thought there would be a woman whose future he cared about so deeply.

And what would her future be? Even if Brad was sent to prison and she returned to her trailer, she was still going to be a single mother struggling to survive alone and on a salary as a grocery store checker.

Who was going to rock her baby in big, sturdy arms? Who was going to be a strong male role model? Flint knew what it was like to grow up without a father and he worried for her and the innocent baby she carried.

He would hope she'd eventually find that cowboy who could be a father to her child and love Madison to distraction. But how difficult was it going to be for her to even date?

She'd have a baby and a job and if that wasn't enough she had the specter of Brad hanging over her. Was it possible the young men in town would believe she made up the accusations against Brad? Would they then be afraid to date her?

"Flint?" Mac's voice yanked him out of his thoughts.

He stared at his friend. "I'm sorry, did you say something to me?"

"Yeah, I asked you three times why you were so quiet," Mac replied.

"Uh…just thinking of that chicken-fried steak," he replied.

"And speaking of…" Madison said as Carlee arrived with the food.

The meal was pleasant despite the occasional glowers that friends of the Ainsworth family cast in their direction. Thankfully, Madison appeared oblivious to the glares. Besides, much to Madison's amusement, Mac and Jerod provided comic relief by reminding Flint of every dumb-ass thing he'd ever done while growing up.

After the meal they stepped out of the café and

nearly bumped into Margery Martin, the president of the Bitterroot Bank. Margery's thin upper lip rose at one corner as she gazed at Madison.

"Maddy, why are you saying such terrible things about that nice young man Brad Ainsworth? What is wrong with you, young lady?" Her beady brown eyes glared at Madison.

Before Flint could move closer to Madison in an effort to somehow shield her, Mac flung his arm around her shoulder. "Come on, Maddy."

"Answer me, Maddy. It's disgraceful. Why are you lying about all this?" Margery pressed.

"I'm not lying. Brad beat me and then he raped me, and that's the truth," Madison replied, her voice trembling.

"You will burn in hell for your lying, young lady," Margery exclaimed as Mac guided Madison away from the vicious old woman.

"Don't mind her," Jerod said when they reached Flint's truck. "She's nothing but an old biddy."

"Yeah, maybe we could start a little rumor about her," Jerod said. "We could whisper to people that she has a secret sex cave in her basement and she whips men's butts for money."

Flint had never loved his friends as much as he did now, when he heard Madison giggle. She sobered once they were all loaded back into the truck and headed back to the Holiday Ranch.

"I knew there would be people who didn't believe me," Madison said. "But I never thought about another woman coming after me like that."

"Keep in mind Margery has always been uptight and judgmental and she's also very close friends with the Ainsworths," Flint said.

"Even with all the stares and the whispering, I'm glad we got out," she replied.

Flint wondered how she might have handled it if they had run into Brad? And how would Brad handle seeing her? Would the man be civil? Somehow, Flint thought so. There was no way Brad would let his mask of being a good, upstanding man slip so that anyone else might see the monster beneath.

It took only minutes for Jerod and Mac to get out of the truck and then Flint and Madison were alone as they drove back to the cabin.

As he drove, he kept an eye on the rearview mirror. He knew Brad drove a big white Cadillac, a car that would be easy to spot if it was following them. Flint saw no vehicle behind them that gave him any pause.

Now all he had to do was keep his distance from Madison and make sure she didn't wind up in his bed again.

Brad stood in the front window of his insurance agency and stared out at Main Street. People ambled up and down the sidewalks, smiling as they went about their daily business.

He knew people were talking about him since that bitch Maddy had come forward, but he was satisfied by the fact that the rumble on the streets was that he was the victim of a vindictive woman.

He had plenty of support. Still, he couldn't take the chance that charges would be brought and he'd have to stand trial. Something had to happen before a trial ensued.

He was confident that he would win a court case, but he'd be damned if he wanted to pay for a good defense lawyer and go through all the hassle that a trial would bring.

Thank God he had friends in low places, friends he kept on a secret payroll, friends who would do his dirty work for him. And Brad had dirty work to do.

Fred Gunner, one of those friends, had seen Flint leaving the Holiday Ranch with Maddy in his truck. Fred had followed and discovered a cozy little cabin in the woods.

Brad needed this criminal investigation and the accusations to go away, and the way to do that was to make Maddy go away. If Flint became collateral damage, then so be it.

He smiled and turned away from the window. Now he knew where she was and all he had to do was come up with a plan that assured his own survival.

Chapter 9

Hands pushed her onto the floor and she landed hard. Frantically, she skittered backward like a crab as he advanced on her. She couldn't breathe... the panic inside her stole her ability to draw air into her lungs.

No...no...no! Her brain screamed in horrified protest. What was happening? Why was he doing this to her? He reared back with his leg and then kicked her, the blow to her ribs torching a white-hot pain through her.

She'd always thought he was nice, that he was a good guy. All she'd wanted was a ride home. She'd never dreamed this could happen.

He laughed, a loud, barking noise. The sound was so at odds with what was happening to her that she realized in that moment he was utterly mad. His evil gleefully echoed within the walls of her small trailer and she was alone...so alone with his madness.

His voice was thunder and his eyes flashed with the lightning of a thousand storms. She kicked at him, but he managed to capture her ankles in his hands.

"That's it, fight me, Maddy. I love it when you fight me," he said.

He laughed once again and then he fell on her, his breath hot pants of excitement against her face. It was only then that a scream released from her, a scream that went on and on and...

"Madison. Madison...honey. Wake up, you're having a nightmare."

The deep, familiar voice pierced through the horror and Madison awakened with a gasp. She jolted straight up and into Flint's arms. A deep sob ripped from the very depths of her as she hid her face in the sleepy warmth of the crook of his neck.

"Shhh, it's okay," he murmured into her hair as his hand caressed up and down her back. "It's okay, honey. You're safe here with me, Madison."

As her sobs began to subside, she realized it was storming outside. Apparently, the thunder and light-

ning of the storm overhead had invaded her nightmare about Brad.

Even though she had stopped crying, she continued to cling to Flint. He smelled of sweet familiarity and of safety. He warmed away the icy chill not
only of her body, but also in the depths of her soul.

It was finally he who dropped his arms from
around her. Gently, he ran his fingers across her
cheeks to dry her tears. "You okay now?" he asked.

She shook her head. "No, I don't like the storm.
Spend the rest of the night here with me?"

He hesitated. "The storm has almost passed. I'll
stay with you until you fall asleep again." He patted the pillow. "Now, get comfortable."

She lay back, disappointed that he wasn't going
to crawl beneath the sheets with her and snuggle
through the rest of the night. "Tell me a story, Flint.
At least talk to me until I fall back asleep." She
needed to fill her head with something...with anything other than her nightmare images about the
monster who had violated her.

Flint started talking about big Cass and when
he'd first arrived on the Holiday Ranch as a frightened thirteen-year-old with no real future. He told
her about Cass welcoming them to her home, to a
different kind of stable lifestyle that none of them
had had before.

She wanted to hear all the things he had to say,

but his low, smooth voice was so hypnotic and within minutes she knew no more.

Madison awoke to the scent of fresh coffee and frying bacon. She jerked up in alarm and then remembered that Flint was here. She wasn't accustomed to him being in the cabin in the mornings.

She relaxed back into the bed and stared up at the ceiling. She fought against a shiver as she remembered the nightmare that had stolen her peaceful sleep. Thank God Flint had been here to awaken her when he had. She hadn't wanted to relive what else had happened to her at Brad's hands.

However, she wished Flint would have crawled into bed with her. She wished he would have spooned around her with his warm skin and his scent that smelled of home.

She suspected why he hadn't. He'd probably been afraid that if they had shared the same bed for any length of time they would have made love again. And he'd been right to be afraid.

Oh, she wanted him again. She wanted to feel his tender touches on her, to hear the sound of her name as he whispered it. With a sigh of frustration she pulled herself up and out of bed.

After a brief shower she tried to pull on a pair of jeans only to discover she could no longer fasten them over her growing baby bump.

Sooner rather than later she needed to get in and see a doctor. But she still was reluctant for anyone in town to know she was pregnant with Brad's child. At least she had gotten the prenatal vitamins and was now taking them regularly.

She opted for one of her long, flowy dresses and then went out into the kitchen where Flint stood in front of the stove. He turned and greeted her with a smile that warmed her from head to toe.

"Good morning," he said and then turned back to where he was taking bacon out of a skillet.

"And a good morning to you," she replied. She went to the cabinet with the cups and pulled one out for herself. She then grabbed a tea bag and heated water in the microwave.

"Are you hungry?"

The sight of him in his worn, low-riding jeans and the white T-shirt that looked so breathtakingly sexy as it tugged across his broad shoulders definitely made her hungry, but not for anything he was cooking.

"I can always eat bacon," she replied as she carried the hot water and the tea bag to the table.

"How about some scrambled eggs to go with the bacon?"

"Sounds good."

She sipped her tea and watched as he grabbed the eggs and milk from the refrigerator. He broke the eggs into a bowl, added milk and then mixed them together.

Her gaze went to his biceps, then across the

broadness of his back and downward to his tight butt. He turned and looked at her expectantly.

Her cheeks warmed as she realized he must have said something that she didn't hear because she'd been too busy admiring his physical attributes. "I'm sorry?"

"I need to get some groceries so I'll probably leave right after we have breakfast," he said. He placed bread slices in the toaster and then poured the egg mixture into the awaiting skillet. "I shouldn't be gone long. We just need a few things."

"I'll go with you," she replied.

He turned from the stove to look at her once again. "Are you sure you're up to it?"

"I think the more I'm seen in town, maybe the faster the gossip will die down."

He frowned. "Maybe, but have you considered that in coming and going from here Brad will know about this cabin sooner rather than later?"

Madison's chest tightened with tension. She drew in a deep breath and nodded. "I know, but I trust we can remain safe here no matter what." What she really meant was she had complete trust in his ability to protect her from the bogeyman.

She thought about her nightmare the night before. "Thank you for comforting me last night."

"No problem." He buttered the toast, put the bacon and scrambled eggs on plates and then joined her at the table. "Do you have nightmares often?"

"Way too often," she admitted. "And they're always pretty much the same. They're always me reliving what Brad did to me."

"I'm sorry, Madison." His eyes held such tenderness. "I'm so damned sorry that happened to you." Their gazes remained locked for a long, breathless moment. He cleared his throat and gestured toward the plate in front of her. "Now eat, I'm sure Baby Madison is hungry."

It was the first time he'd made such a definite reference to the baby she carried, and a reminder of why Flint probably wouldn't want to be with her. What man would want to take on the burden of a baby who wasn't his?

"Baby Madison is getting bigger and bigger every day," she said, shoving aside any sad thoughts that tried to intrude.

"You really should see a doctor to make sure everything is okay. If you make an appointment I'll be more than happy to take you."

"I'm so afraid Brad will find out, and if he does I know he'll fight me for custody just to hurt me." She couldn't imagine any baby, especially hers, being raised by Brad with his twisted, sick brain.

"Hopefully, he's going to jail soon, but there is no reason why we couldn't have a confidential talk with one of the doctors in town and make an appointment for late at night. There are several doctors I would trust with this secret. The law prevents a doctor from talking about anyone's medical condition without permission."

Madison's hand fell over her tummy. Flint was right. She needed to see a doctor. She loved the baby growing inside her and therefore wanted to get the best possible medical attention she could. She was almost four months pregnant now and it was time to see a doctor.

She hoped that Flint was right and whatever doctor she chose to see would keep her condition a secret. There would come a time when she wouldn't be able to hide her pregnancy any longer, but she prayed that Brad would be arrested well before then.

"Maybe when we get back from grocery shopping we can decide on which doctor I should see."

He grinned at her. "Good. All I want is for you and the baby to be healthy."

While they ate breakfast they talked about the different doctors in town and who would be the best choice. When they finished eating they cleaned up the kitchen and got ready to leave for the grocery store in town.

Once again over her sleeveless dress she pulled on the blue sweater that hid her baby bump from view. Eventually, the sweater wouldn't be able to cover her pregnancy. And certainly pretty soon she was going to have to buy some maternity clothes. Oh, the gossip that would start then.

She didn't want to think of any of that right now. All she wanted to do was go out with Flint. Even if it was only for a trip to the grocery store, she looked forward to doing something normal like food shopping with him.

"Ready?" Flint asked.

She looked at him in surprise. He had on a shoulder holster with a gun nestled inside. "That both scares me and comforts me," she said.

"I doubt if I ever need to use it," he replied. "But cowboys are like Boy Scouts…always prepared."

"You didn't wear it when we went to the café," she replied.

"True, but if you remember both Mac and Jerod were armed."

"Well, I like that being prepared part about you," she replied with a grin. Together they left the cabin and got into his truck. She buckled in and they took off.

"What the hell…" He slowed the truck. Ahead of them, in the middle of the narrow lane, several large branches blocked their path.

"Maybe the storm last night blew down the branches," she said.

"Maybe…" he replied. He pulled the truck up closer to the obstruction in their path. Several loud popping noises suddenly broke the silence. Madison screamed as her window exploded inward.

* * *

"Get down! Get down!" Flint yelled to Madison. The bullets were coming from somebody hiding in the woods on the right side of the road, but there was no way Flint could return fire, not with Madison between him and the shooter. As Madison curled into the seat he threw the truck into Reverse and gunned the engine.

He sped backward and screeched to a halt at the cabin's front door. He jumped out of the driver side, drew his gun and then went around to the passenger side.

He helped Madison out of the truck and shielded her as they raced for the front door. He unlocked the door and pushed her inside. "Get in the bathroom and lock the door. Don't come out until I tell you to."

He turned back around and stood at the door, gun ready for anyone who might approach. Nobody was going to get through him to hurt Madison... nobody! He listened for any rustling in the woods and narrowed his gaze as he surveyed the area.

Dammit, his words to Madison about being prepared ran through his mind as if to mock him. He certainly hadn't been prepared for this attack. Even when he'd seen the branches in the middle of the road, initially he'd had no thought of impending danger.

Dammit, he should have been prepared for anything and he hadn't been. Thank God the bullet that had blown through Madison's window hadn't hit her. His chest tightened at the very thought of her being hurt in any way.

He wasn't sure how long he stood there, like a sentry guarding the princess. He finally went into the cabin and directly to his phone in his bedroom. His cell phone was fairly worthless out here in the woods, but with his landline he called Dillon and told him what happened.

When he hung up he hurried back to the front door and resumed his position on the porch. At least he knew that in the windowless bathroom Madison would be safe from any flying bullets that might come.

He had no idea if the shooter had been alone or if there were others. But no matter who came out of the woods to approach the cabin, Flint would shoot first and ask questions later.

As time ticked by he suspected whoever had attacked them was gone. He didn't sense anyone lurking in the woods as birds resumed singing in the treetops.

Within minutes the sound of an approaching siren pierced the air. The siren stopped and Flint knew Dillon had probably reached the blockade of branches.

Several minutes later Dillon's patrol car drove

up and parked next to Flint's truck. Dillon got out, as well as officers David Cook and Clint Graham.

The two officers walked back down the lane as Dillon joined Flint. "Let's go inside and you can tell me exactly what happened."

"First, I need to get Madison out of the bathroom. I sent her in there because I didn't know if somebody was going to open fire on the cabin." Flint opened the front door and the two men went inside.

Flint immediately went to the bathroom and knocked on the door. "Madison, Dillon is here. You can come out now."

The door opened and she flew into his arms. Her warm curves fit perfectly against him as she clung to him. A soft sob escaped her and more than anything Flint wished he could take away the fear that he knew she was experiencing. She had to have been terrified when the bullet shattered her window.

He reluctantly released her and guided her to the sofa where she sat. Flint sank down next to her as Dillon sat on the chair opposite them. "Now," he said. "Tell me exactly what happened."

"We were headed to town to do some grocery shopping." As Flint told Dillon what had occurred, he was aware of Madison leaning into him.

"Did you get a look at the shooter?" Dillon asked when Flint was finished.

"No, whoever shot at us was completely hidden from view."

"You know it was Brad," Madison interjected. "It has to be him. Since I've told what he did to me, he now wants me dead." Her voice trembled with emotion.

"I'm not going to let that happen," Flint said. He wrapped his arm around her shoulder and she nestled even closer to his side, but he could still feel her trembling.

Dillon asked a few more questions and then the two officers came in the front door. "We checked the area and there's nobody hiding out in the woods right now," Officer Graham said.

"But we did find a place where the grass was tamped down, indicating that somebody was hiding there," he added.

"The coward shot at us and then ran," Flint said with disgust.

"We'll try to get some slugs out of your car so we at least know what kind of gun was used. We'll then head back into town and check out where Brad was at during the time of the attack," Dillon said. He stood. "In the meantime, you're on notice that somebody is not happy with you," he said to Flint.

"I'll warn you that if it comes to it I'll shoot to kill." Flint stood, as well. "And I hope Brad is in jail for attempted murder before nightfall."

"Walk us out?" Dillon asked.

Flint nodded and together the three men stepped outside. "I didn't want to say too much in front of Maddy," Dillon said as his other men got back into the patrol car.

"I appreciate that," Flint replied. "She's pretty shaken up by this."

"As she should be. We both know those bullets were meant for her. They came through the passenger side of the truck and not through your side," Dillon said.

"Brad has to be behind this," Flint said. "Nothing else makes any sense."

"I know that and you know that. Now I've got to see if I can prove it." Dillon's jaw tightened as he gazed around. "You're pretty isolated out here. You're going to have to be on your toes because I can't provide you much in the way of support and protection this far from town."

"Trust me. I'll be on my toes."

They both turned as Madison stepped out on the porch. "We're still going into town for groceries," she said. Her chin lifted as she walked over to the passenger side of his truck. "I'll just clean out the glass and then we'll be on our way."

Her voice was strained and her movements jerky, completely unlike her. Flint stopped her from opening the truck door. "Madison, we can get groceries another day or I can have somebody pick them up and bring them to us."

"No." She whirled away from Flint. "He doesn't get to win. He's not going to make me be a prisoner here. I told you before. He's taken enough from me. He doesn't get to say I can't go to the grocery store. He's not going to take away all my freedom." Her eyes flashed with defiance as she glared first at Flint and then at Dillon.

"If I end up dead, then I want you to do whatever is in your power to see that Brad Ainsworth goes to prison for my rape and murder." Her defiance began to melt away. Her shoulders sagged and her eyes filled with tears. She began to visibly tremble.

"Madison." Flint said her name softly and moved to pull her into a comforting embrace. But with a small gasp, she jerked away from him, turned and ran back into the cabin.

"I'd better get in there," Flint said with a worried look toward the front door.

"We'll see what we can find on your truck and I'll be in touch with any information I get," Dillon replied. As he motioned for the other two officers to join him at his truck, Flint hurried into the house.

He found Madison on her bed, sobbing into her pillow. He sank down on the bed next to her. "Madison, I know you're scared." He rubbed his hand up and down her back. "But everything is going to be okay."

She jerked up and angrily wiped the tears off her face. "Damn right I'm scared." Her eyes blazed an icy blue. "I'm scared and I'm sorry I ever said anything about this at all. I should have just kept my mouth shut about everything that monster did to me."

She scooted to the end of the bed and then left the bedroom. He knew those moments in the truck with somebody shooting at them had scared her. The sudden and unexpected attack had scared the hell out of him.

He hurried after her, confused by the mixed messages she was sending. She stood in the living room, staring out the front window, and that was the last place he wanted her standing.

"Madison," he said softly. "Come away from the window and tell me what I can do to help you get through this."

Thankfully, she stepped away from the window and then turned to look at him. She looked so sad... so utterly broken and he hated seeing her that way.

She released a deep, tremulous sigh. "I intend to call Dillon and tell him I don't want to pursue this. I'll tell him that I just made it all up. That it didn't really happen and I... I was just looking for attention."

"Madison, don't make that kind of decision right now when you're so scared. Come sit with me."

She paused a long moment and then moved across the floor to sit on the chair. Flint sat on the sofa facing her. "Now that we know Brad is stupid enough to want to hurt you, I'll be on my toes. I misread the situation earlier, but I won't make the same mistake again. I swear I can keep you safe."

She wrapped her arms around herself as if chilled to the very bone. He was vaguely surprised by his need to grab her up into a tight embrace.

He wanted to hold her until she was no longer cold with her thoughts of attempted murder and Brad. But she'd chosen to sit in the chair where he couldn't sit next to her and there was absolutely nothing about her demeanor that invited him to draw her into his arms.

"Talk to me, Madison." He needed to know what was going on in her head.

"I have nothing more to say about any of it. I'm done. I intend to call Dillon first thing in the morning and call the whole thing off." Her voice was small and hopeless, and it broke Flint's heart for her.

"Could you give it a little more time before you do that?" he asked. Maybe if she could get a little bit of distance from the shooting, she would feel stronger.

She frowned and tightened her arms around her waist. "It won't make a difference. I'm not going to change my mind."

"Would you just give it a week?" He figured maybe within that time some of the terror of the attack that morning would dissipate and she would make a better decision.

Up to this point she had been so determined to get Brad behind bars for his crimes against her. The man *needed* to be rotting away somewhere in a prison.

She released a weary sigh. "Okay, I'll see how I feel about things tomorrow," she finally replied.

It wasn't exactly what he wanted to hear, but it would have to be enough for now. He rose. "If you'll be all right, I'm going to go out and clean up my truck. I also need to call Larry Wright at the car dealership and see if he can get me a window replacement as soon as possible."

She waved a hand in the direction of the door. "Go, do whatever you need to do. I think I'm going to take a nap." She pulled herself out of the chair and then disappeared into her bedroom.

A wave of helplessness shot through him. He'd been unable to stop the attack that morning from happening. He was now unable to make her feel safe enough to pursue her charges against Brad. And now she wasn't even allowing him to comfort her.

Minutes later he was outside with a shop vacuum and a trash bag. As he ran the vac to pick up the small shards of glass that sparkled in the sunlight, his thoughts were filled with Madison.

He was worried about her. She just appeared

so…so fragile and so very broken right now. He wanted to help her, but he didn't know how.

There was no way he could feel what she felt. There was no way he could put himself in her skin. He wanted to support her, but he hoped she continued on with the case against Brad. Even if she decided not to pursue the case he would still support her.

He finished the cleanup and put the shop vacuum back in the garage and then went back inside the cabin. It was quiet and Madison was no place in sight. Her bedroom door was partially open and he peeked in on her.

She was asleep, her dark, beautiful hair fanned out on the white pillowcase. She seemed to be completely at ease, her delicate features not indicating any bad dreams.

Good. He wanted her to have happy dreams. He wanted…he wished…he stepped back from the door and half stumbled to the nearby chair.

He collapsed down, half-breathless with the sudden and shocking realization that he was madly, crazy in love with her.

Chapter 10

Madison sat on the sofa with a book in her hand, but her brain was so involved in the chaos of her thoughts, it couldn't compute the words on the pages.

A week had gone by since the shooting and there had been no more trouble since then. However, she and Flint had remained holed up in the cabin during the past seven days.

She had done nothing to advance or halt the charge against Brad. Dillon had called the day after the shooting and had told Dillon that Brad had been alibied for the time of the attack by his long-term girlfriend, Cindy Carter.

Cindy had told Dillon that Brad had spent the

night with her and during the time of the incident he and Cindy had been having a leisurely breakfast together.

There seemed to be no way to prove Brad's guilt and Madison was just sick of the whole thing. Dillon had called twice more to speak with her, but she had refused to take the phone calls.

She was definitely sorry she had come forward in the first place and now just wanted it to all go away. A dozen times she had thought about calling Dillon and telling him to drop the whole thing. She still intended to make the call; she just hadn't done it yet.

She should have just followed through on her initial plan to keep her mouth shut and leave town. She should have climbed on a bus the next day after her car had broken down.

But then she wouldn't have gotten to know Flint. She wouldn't have known the joy of laughing with him. She wouldn't have known the happiness of being held in his arms, or the absolute wonder of making love with him. She couldn't and wouldn't wish any of that away.

Although ultimately she knew Flint would support her in whatever she decided to do about Brad, he'd been acting strange all week. He had been rather distant and quiet and in the evenings he'd taken to sitting in the chair rather than next to her on the sofa. He was also spending most of the days working outside around the place.

Restlessly, she now got up from the table and walked over to the front window. Flint was just outside, painting the porch with a sealant.

Her heart expanded as she watched him work. He looked so strong, so capable of handling anything that came his way. But she had seen the expression of pain that sometimes raced across his features. She had watched him in the evenings rubbing his hands as if there was an ache deep inside them.

She supposed it was just what he'd told her, that it was old, broken bones aching. But she hated seeing him in any kind of pain. There was no question in her mind that he'd saved her life by offering her this warm and wonderful shelter.

Who knew where she'd be right now if not for him? Getting on a bus and leaving Bitterroot might have ended in horrible circumstances.

With a deep sigh she moved from the window to the kitchen table with her book in hand. Once again she felt more than a bit of cabin fever. There was no question that the attack in the truck had scared her, but how long was she going to remain holed up in here? How long did she allow her fear to keep her a virtual captive?

She looked up as Flint came through the door.

He smiled at her, the smile that cast a warmth over her. "How are you doing?"

"Okay." She watched as he washed his hands in the sink and then moved to the coffeemaker. He popped the pod in and then turned back to look at her.

"You said you're okay, but you don't sound okay. You sound a little depressed."

She released another deep sigh. "I think I want to try it again."

He frowned in obvious confusion. "Try what again?"

"Leaving here…going into town. Maybe we could have dinner at the café this evening."

He got his coffee and then sat across the table from her. "Sounds good to me, but are you sure you're up to it?"

She hesitated a moment and then nodded her head. "I need to be up to it. I don't like feeling as if I'm imprisoned by my own fear."

"Madison, I'm up for whatever you want to do and I'll do my best to make sure you stay safe."

He looked so earnest and so determined. Her heart swelled with emotions she'd never felt before about a man…emotions too great for her to deal with at the moment. Instead, she simply smiled at him. "Then let's go out for dinner."

"That sounds like a plan to me."

An awkward silence fell between them, one that

had become far too familiar over the past week. She wasn't sure exactly what had changed between them, but something definitely had.

Maybe it had been her decision not to pursue the charges against Brad that had changed Flint's attitude toward her. She wanted to be strong, but nobody knew the raw, terrifying fear she still harbored toward Brad. Nobody had been in the trailer with her to see what a terrifying monster he had become. And the bullets that had obviously been meant for her only increased her fear of the man. What more could he be capable of?

"Do you want to plan to go in about an hour or so?" Flint asked, breaking the silence that had grown between them.

"That sounds perfect," she replied. "I'm already working up a big appetite."

He smiled at her. "Well, you are eating for two."

Self-consciously she wrapped her arms around her growing waistline. "It's getting more and more difficult to hide. Thank goodness I still have a few loose-fitting dresses."

"You always look beautiful," he replied. His gaze held hers for a long moment and then he stared down into his cup and cleared his throat. "I think I'll head to the shower." He drained the last of his coffee, set the cup in the sink and then disappeared into the bathroom.

She inhaled, the breath hitching in the back of

her throat. For just a moment she'd thought she'd seen something wonderful, something so soft and magical in the forest-green depths of his eyes.

She wanted to rush to him and confess that she was in love with him. She wanted to tell him that she wanted to live in this enchanted cabin in the woods with him forever.

Her heart crashed down to the pit of her pregnant stomach. Maybe she'd only imagined that look in his eyes. Maybe that was what she wanted to see but it hadn't really been there.

He'd brought her into his home because she'd desperately needed a place to stay. He'd been kind enough to allow her to remain here until she got back on her feet.

That didn't mean he was madly in love with her. It only meant he was a man with compassion. She'd checked him out dozens of times while working in the grocery store and he had never expressed an interest in her.

True, he'd made sweet love with her, but having sex with a woman was very different from having real true love for her. There was no question that he was physically attracted to her, that they were physically attracted to each other, but that didn't mean he wanted her in his life forever.

She couldn't tell Flint how she felt about him. She wasn't going to make herself that vulnerable. She already felt vulnerable enough in her life.

She'd been humiliated first by her father, who had been unable to love her and then by Brad's attack. She couldn't stand it if she told Flint her feelings and humiliated herself only for her love to be rejected by him. It was best if she just kept her feelings for him to herself.

Gazing over at the clock on the wall, she pulled herself up and out of the kitchen chair and went into her bedroom to change clothes and put on a little makeup for dinner out.

As she got ready she tried to tamp down the simmering of fear inside her. When they tried to leave the lane would more bullets fly at them? Was Brad waiting for them, hoping to get another opportunity to shoot her?

While they were driving into town would somebody try to run them off the road, or fire bullets from another car with the intent of hopefully killing her? When they left the café to get into the truck to come home would somebody come at them out of the shadows of the night?

She had so much more to live for now with the baby growing inside her. The baby was an innocent soul and didn't deserve to die for Madison's actions.

She sank down on the edge of the bed and moved her hands across her stomach in a caressing motion. She didn't know what might happen, but somehow, someway, she needed to assure her baby a future.

Once again she thought the best course of action might be to not only ignore the investigation of Brad but actually recant her accusations against him. Maybe that would assure not only her safety, but that of her baby's, too.

She shoved these troubling thoughts away. She needed to finish up dressing, otherwise Flint would be waiting for her. She finally proclaimed herself ready and left the bedroom.

Flint stood at the front window and turned as he heard her approach. "You look really nice," he said.

"Thank you. You clean up rather well yourself." Actually he cleaned up more than well. He looked totally hot in his jeans and a navy Polo shirt that made his slightly shaggy hair appear blonder than usual.

He wore his shoulder holster and grabbed a light-weight navy blue jacket and put it on. What a couple they made…his jacket hid his gun and her sweater hid her growing baby bump.

Still, for a moment she fantasized they were a real couple going out for a nice dinner after a long day. They would visit with friends and talk about silly stuff and laugh together and then come home and make sweet love.

"I'm going to make a quick run down the lane by myself and then I'll come back to get you," he said.

His words instantly shattered the fantasy as she was jerked back to the here and now and her current situation. "Then I'll just wait for you in here."

A few minutes later she watched as Flint's truck drove away from the cabin and disappeared from view. Nerves jumped inside her and anxiety grew as she waited for him to return. Her concerns mounted with each minute that ticked by. Finally, relief fluttered through her as he came back into view. He pulled to a halt in front of her and waited for her to climb into the passenger seat.

"Everything seems to be quiet," he said.

"Quiet is good." She pulled her seat belt around her and fastened it as he took off back down the lane. Her heart quickened its rhythm as they reached the spot where the bullets had flown at her a week before.

They passed the spot without incident and continued on to the road that would lead to Bitterroot. Finally, she relaxed back into the seat.

She rolled down her window and drew in a deep breath of the fresh air. "It feels good to be out again," she said. Thankfully, Larry Wright had come to the cabin a day after the shooting with two men and a new window for Flint's truck.

"It does," he agreed. "It's a beautiful evening."

It was indeed a gorgeous evening. The sky was a clear blue without a cloud to be had. The sun hung low in the western sky and promised a stunning sunset.

"I can't imagine prettier sunsets in any other

place in the world than what we have here in Oklahoma," she said.

"I definitely agree with that," he replied. "Hopefully, there will be beautiful sunsets wherever you eventually wind up if you decide to leave Bitterroot."

She didn't reply. Certainly, there was no way she could remain here now that she'd come forward with her accusation of Brad. As long as he freely walked the streets of the town she couldn't remain here.

Even if she recanted now, which she was leaning toward doing, he'd still make it impossible for her to remain here. She would always be afraid of repercussions. And what might he do when he found out she had a baby?

His family had plenty of money and she seriously doubted she could fight them if it came to a custody battle. They would make her out to be an unfit mother and she wouldn't have the resources to fight them.

It didn't escape her that the baby would be proof positive that something sexual had happened between them, but she wasn't about to use the baby to prove her case. Besides, Brad would just lie and say that the sex between them had been consensual.

She fought against a heavy veil of depression that threatened to fall over her. She was so confused about everything going on in her life.

"You're very quiet." Flint broke through her thoughts.

"I'm overthinking things," she confessed.

He cast her a quick glance. "Stop doing that. It causes you to frown and I want you looking forward to dinner out with a smile on your face."

Despite her earlier thoughts, his words caused a smile. "Okay, I'll stop. I really am looking forward to dinner out."

"Is there anything you're particularly hungry for?"

She thought about all the offerings on the café menu. "I think I want a juicy cheeseburger with a side of fries. And then for dessert maybe a piece of that chocolate cake with the salty caramel frosting."

He laughed. "That sounds like a tall order for a little bit like you."

"Ah, but remember I'm eating for two."

He laughed again, and she wondered if she would ever grow tired of the rich, deep sound. "What are you looking forward to ordering?"

"Spaghetti…with a couple of meatballs on the side."

"Ah, someday I'll make you my homemade sauce and I'll make meatballs that will knock your socks off," she replied.

"Sounds good to me," he replied.

They fell silent as they entered the town. The parking spaces in front of the café were already filled with cars and trucks and he had to find a spot a half a block away.

"Sit tight, I'll come around to let you out," he said once they were parked.

She waited and once she was out of the truck, Flint flung an arm around her shoulder and pulled her close to his side. While she wished it was love that had him being so affectionate, she knew he was protecting her from the potential danger that might come at them while they were exposed on the sidewalk.

He dropped his arm from around her as they entered the busy café. At least in here they could both relax because the odds of anyone coming after her were minimal with all the other diners as witnesses.

Once again she was aware of the whispers and gazes that followed them as they moved to an empty booth in the back. What were they all saying about her? What did they believe about her? She raised her chin as if to ward off any judgment that might come her way.

He gestured her toward the seat that would have her back to most of the other people in the café while he sat across from her, facing those people and the front door.

They had been seated for only a couple of minutes when Becky Davis, a pretty young brunette, came to wait on them. "How are you all this evening?" she asked as she handed them menus. She smiled at Madison. "Maddy, you look real pretty. That blue sweater is really nice on you."

"Thanks," Madison replied in surprise. At least there was one person in town who could still be nice to her. Hopefully, there were others.

"Tell me what you all want to drink and then I'll be back to get your food orders," Becky said.

Minutes later they had their drinks and Becky had taken their food orders. "I don't think the gawkers are as bad this time as the last time we came here," she said.

He smiled. "We don't care about gawkers or gossipers, do we?"

She shook her head. She didn't care about much of anything when he smiled at her with that special something in his eyes that sluiced a sweet warmth through her. He held her gaze for a long moment and then looked down at his drink.

Why was it that there were times when he looked at her that she thought she saw love in the depths of his eyes? And then other times she saw a distance there that felt insurmountable.

Confusion about Flint aside, there was no question that she was still considered some kind of pariah. They had passed several people she knew when they'd come in, but nobody stopped by their booth to say hello.

Although it bothered her a bit, it bothered her more for Flint. She'd seen him when he came into the grocery store and had noticed how often he was greeted and stopped to chat for a few minutes by other shoppers. He'd been so well liked before all this, and now nobody was talking to him because he was with her.

"Hey, there's that frown again." His deep voice broke through her thoughts.

"Sorry. I was just thinking how nobody has talked to you since we got here and I know it's all my fault. If you weren't here with me I know people would be stopping by to greet you and talk to you."

"Do I look upset? Madison, I don't care about the people who don't talk to me. I care about my friends, who believe in what I'm doing and believe your claims. I care about you and I'm not going to lose any sleep because these acquaintances decided not to talk to me. Now, no more frowning for the rest of the night, deal?"

"Deal," she replied. How did she get so lucky to have Flint on her side? He was so comfortable in his own skin, so sure about his friendships and what he was doing in his life. He would never know the depth of her admiration for him.

At that moment Becky returned to the booth with their dinner orders. "Mmm, these fries are heavenly," she said a few minutes later. She dragged another one of the potatoes through a pool of ketchup and then popped it into her mouth. "I figure it's one for me and then one for the baby."

Flint grinned at her. "So what you're telling me is you're really only taking personal responsibility for eating half of the fries."

"Exactly," she replied with a laugh.

"What do you want? A boy or a girl?"

"I don't care. As long as the baby is healthy that's all that really matters."

"Which reminds me, we need to get you a doctor appointment. Have you decided who you want to see?" Flint swirled his fork in his spaghetti and then took a bite.

"I'm leaning toward Dr. Clayton Rivers. I know he delivered a baby for McKenzie Warren, who used to work at the grocery store, and she was really pleased with him."

"Clayton is my doctor and I like him," Flint replied. "I'm sure we can trust him. Tomorrow I'll call and see if we can get you set up with a late-night appointment. I'm also certain he will respect your privacy and not gossip about your condition."

"Hey, you two. I didn't know you had plans to eat out this evening," Mac said as he appeared by their booth.

"We didn't know it until about an hour before we came," Madison replied.

"What are you doing here instead of having dinner at the ranch?" Flint asked his friend.

"Cookie served up sloppy joes tonight so I talked Jerod into coming here for dinner," Mac replied.

Flint laughed. "You never did like Cookie's sloppy joes."

"I don't know what it is, but he uses something in the sauce I don't like. We're headed to the Watering Hole after we eat. Do you two want to tag along?"

Oh, there was nothing Madison would like more than to head to the most popular bar in town. They could listen to the music and then perhaps Flint would take her in his arms, hold her close and move her around the dance floor.

"Thanks, but with the way things are right now I think it's best we just head on home after we eat," Flint replied.

"I'm keeping you from doing the things you like to do," Madison said when Mac had moved away from their booth.

"What? Going to the Watering Hole? There were plenty of nights I stayed home when the rest of the cowboys would head to the bar for drinking and dancing. I've never been a big drinker. Not going isn't a big loss for me, Madison." He smiled at her reassuringly. "Now, how about I get Becky over here to take our dessert order? I believe you wanted a big piece of that chocolate cake."

She looked down at her nearly empty plate and then patted her stomach. "Oh, I don't know. It sounded good before I ate a big cheeseburger and all those fries. I'm pretty full right now."

"I'm going to order a piece of apple pie and some coffee."

"Oh, what the heck, I can stuff in at least a few bites of cake," she replied with a laugh.

Minutes later they had their dessert before them and their conversation turned to favorite desserts. "There's nothing I like better than apple pie," he said.

"I'll make you an apple pie that you'll never forget," she replied confidently. "You should have told me before now that it was one of your favorite desserts."

"You've been making me such good suppers I haven't even thought about dessert. And speaking of that, I need to write you a check that you can put toward getting your car fixed, although I hope you stick around here long enough to see through the charges against Brad."

Every single word he spoke depressed her and reminded her of her position right now. "I told you I might not go through with it. I'm still thinking about recanting and just letting it all go."

"You know I'll support you whatever you decide," he said softly. "But no matter what you do, I hope you talk to somebody to help you with your nightmares."

Once again his gaze held hers and she wanted to fall into the green depths that were so inviting. She didn't want to think about Brad Ainsworth or getting her car fixed. She didn't want to think about leaving Bitterroot. All she wanted to do was go home to the cabin and be with Flint again.

As they finished eating their dessert the conversation grew lighter as he entertained her with stories of the antics of him, Mac and Jerod when they'd been younger.

"The original twelve of us were all close, but Mac and Jerod and I had a deeper friendship. We didn't spend a lot of time talking about our pasts. We worked hard during the days, but when work knocked off for the day we were involved in a lot of mischief."

"Like what?" she asked, as always loving to hear about his time as a kid on Cass's ranch.

"We all knew Sawyer had kind of an OCD issue with his bed. He didn't like wrinkles in his sheets and so the three of us were responsible for sneaking things into his bed."

"Things?"

"Yeah, like dead fish and live frogs and stinky cheese…things like that."

"Oh, Flint, that's terrible," she exclaimed with a laugh.

He grinned. "Yeah, it was pretty rotten of us to do. Eventually, the others got involved and it was still happening until he moved off the ranch."

"Does this mean I need to start checking my bed before I go to sleep at night?"

"No," he replied with a laugh. "I promise you I outgrew that particular kind of mischief."

By this time they had finished eating and Flint paid the tab. Then they left their booth and walked back toward the entrance.

"Bitch," somebody muttered loud enough for her to hear.

"Lying bitch," another male voice half shouted.

"Leave town," yet another male voice said.

She had no idea who had said the hateful things. Even though tears began to burn her eyes, she held her head up high and didn't look left or right. She was conscious of Flint moving closer to her side, but his presence couldn't take away the sting of the hurtful words.

The minute they stepped outside she turned to face Flint. "I want this over. I can't take anymore. As soon as we get home I'm calling Dillon and telling him I lied about Brad."

She whirled around and started down the sidewalk toward where they had parked. She was so over it. She was tired of being judged, of not being able to go out in public without condemnation and threat of death. If she recanted and just left Bitterroot, it would solve everything.

Flint walked beside her and didn't say a word. It was as if he knew her well enough to know when to just be quiet. She also knew he would stand beside her no matter what she did. She just wanted this to all go away.

They reached his truck and there was a folded piece of paper beneath the windshield wiper on the passenger side. She stared at it, a sense of dread sweeping through her.

What now? A death threat in writing? She drew a deep breath and pulled it out from the windshield wiper. Her fingers trembled as she opened it, her vision aided by a nearby streetlight.

Thank you for coming forward. Brad beat and raped me, too.

The bold, dark letters screamed in her head. She'd always suspected it was possible Brad had other victims in town. However, the idea had been abstract in her brain. This note made it real. It was proof positive that there were other victims.

"What is it?" Flint asked.

She handed him the note and at the same time looked around the area. Who had left it for her? What poor, innocent young woman had suffered at Brad's hands just like Madison had?

There was nobody on the street. Had it been somebody who had been in the café with them? A diner? Or maybe one of the young, pretty waitresses? It was obviously somebody who was afraid, otherwise she would have signed the note. And how many other victims were there hiding in the shadows of fear in this town? And how many more potential victims would there be in the future if she didn't do the right thing?

Somebody had to speak up for them. Somebody had to do something in an effort to stop Brad. And if she didn't stop him now then she would be partially responsible for any future victims.

She got into the truck and waited for Flint. He slid behind the steering wheel and started the engine. "Before we go home I want to go to the police station. We need to give this note to Dillon and I need to tell him I'm completely committed to getting Brad behind bars."

"Good girl," Flint murmured and handed the note back to her.

As he pulled out of the parking space and headed down the street toward the police station, her mind cleared for what felt like the first time in weeks.

She'd been so wishy-washy about pursuing the charges against Brad. But the note had given her complete clarity and a strength she didn't know she possessed.

She was ready to face the monster and if she got killed in the process, then at least she would die knowing she did the right thing, not just for herself but for all the victims that existed.

Chapter 11

Flint barely recognized the woman now seated opposite Dillon in his office. Flint had seen Madison scared and he'd seen her crying. He'd seen her angry and he'd seen her happy, but he'd never seen her so coldly determined.

She was calm and controlled as she handed Dillon the note. "We found this on Flint's truck when we left the café a few minutes ago."

Dillon read the note and a muscle began to pulse in his jaw as he set it down on his desk. "Did you see who left it?"

"No, we didn't see anyone on the street who might have left it for me to find," Madison said.

"And I don't suppose you have any idea who left it there?"

"None, but it's obvious from that note that there's another victim of his. And there might be more," Madison said. "Something has to be done about Brad."

"I can't do anything without any solid evidence," Dillon replied in obvious frustration. "If I take a charge to the prosecutor and all I have is a he said-she said situation that happened over three months ago, the odds are he won't go forward."

Dillon picked up the note and frowned thoughtfully. "I need to start interviewing all the young women in town and see if I can find this other victim. If I can find out who she is, then hopefully, I can convince her to come forward. Then I would feel more comfortable that he would be successfully prosecuted."

"You'll let me know what you find out?" Madison asked.

"I will," Dillon replied. "And if anyone contacts you about this, you'll let me know?"

"Of course. All I want is to put this man away where he can't hurt anyone else ever again. I know I haven't been one hundred percent on board with this for the past week, but I'm completely committed to doing whatever it takes to get Brad Ainsworth behind bars." Madison stood and Flint did the same, taking his cues from her.

Moments later they were back in the truck. Before he started the engine she placed her hand on his thigh. "Thank you, Flint."

He thought he could feel the warmth of her hand on him through his jeans. "Thank me for what?" he asked, trying to ignore how much he liked her touch. He'd hungered for it in the past week when he'd been trying to gain some distance from her.

"For putting up with me being so ambivalent about all this." She squeezed his thigh and then moved her hand back to her lap.

"I just wanted you to do whatever you needed to do for your personal peace," he replied and then started the truck engine. "But I have to admit that I'm glad you're committed to going after the bastard."

"That note on the truck made me realize I needed to do everything in my power to stop him. If I don't do it for myself, I need to do it for any other past and future victims." She leaned her head back as he pulled onto the road to go home.

"Are you tired?" he asked. "It's been a fairly eventful night."

"It has been, but I'm not really tired, although I'm ready to get home."

Home. The cabin had truly become the home he'd wished for when he'd been a child. Big Cass and the Holiday Ranch had been a wonderful place for him as a broken kid. He'd had a wonderful upbringing there, but it had never been the soul-satisfying space he now called home.

And he knew much of his happiness and that feeling of home was because of having Madison in his life. When he'd imagined living at the cabin, he'd assumed that the first thing he'd see in the mornings were deer that would come out of the woods.

Instead, he looked forward to seeing Madison in the mornings. He loved drinking his coffee with her across the table from him, with the shimmer of morning sunshine painting her beautiful features in a golden hue.

He looked forward to eating all his meals with her, to settling in during the evenings side by side on the sofa and talking or watching television.

She filled his dreams with the thought of their lovemaking burned in his head at the most inappropriate times…like right now.

With her just sitting next to him in the truck and filling the interior with her scent, he wanted her. She leaned her head back and began to hum a popular country-western song. She often hummed or sang softly, especially when she was in the shower, and he loved the sound of her.

He'd allowed his feelings for her to spin way out of control. He knew they had no future together, but even knowing that he couldn't seem to stop falling deeper and deeper in love with her.

"All I'm looking forward to for the rest of the evening is relaxing on the sofa to watch some television," she said as she stopped humming and he pulled to a halt in front of the cabin.

"Sounds good to me," he replied. They got out and went inside where the first thing she did was take off her sweater. He couldn't help but notice the press of her breasts against her cotton dress.

Jeez, what was wrong with him tonight? He couldn't seem to get sex with Madison off his mind. Maybe if they watched a little TV, he'd be able to shove these thoughts clear out of his head.

A few minutes later a sitcom played and he enjoyed the sound of her laughter. She needed a few laughs after the evening she had endured. While dinner was pleasant with her concentrating on him, he knew the humiliation she had to have felt when they were leaving the café.

He'd led her to the back of the building and had sat her where he had so that she wouldn't have to see the smirks of other diners while she ate. He hadn't thought ahead enough to realize that when they were finished eating, she'd have to face all those people when they walked out.

But she'd done so with dignity and grace. She had held her head high and not responded to the negativity. However, he had wanted to drag some people out in the street and whoop their asses.

Madison was a woman who would fight to the

ends of the earth for those she loved. He knew without doubt her baby would be one of the luckiest children alive. Madison was beautiful inside and out and she had a vibrancy about her that was infinitely appealing. Any man would be proud to claim her as his wife.

A wave of depression descended on him. He'd love to have her in his life and be the father to the baby she carried. He'd love to continue on with what had been already built between them, but that was all a fantasy that would never be.

As if to punctuate that thought his hands ached and his knees began to burn. "I know it's a little early, but I think I'm going to call it a day."

Madison looked at him in surprise. "Are you okay?" she asked worriedly.

"I'm fine," he assured her. "I probably ate too much and now I'm just tired."

"Maybe I should just head to bed, too."

"Only if you want, but if you're worried about the television bothering me…don't. Feel free to stay up as long as you want." He stood and offered her a reassuring smile. "I'll just see you in the morning."

He escaped to his room and closed the door to shuck off his jeans and take off his shirt. When he was clad only in his boxers and with his gun on the nightstand in easy reach he then opened his door halfway.

He never slept with the door closed. He was

a light sleeper and wanted to be able to hear any sound that might indicate trouble. With Madison fully committed to bringing Brad down he didn't know what to expect.

By now Brad probably knew that he and Madison had gone to the chief of police this evening, but there was no way he knew they had a note corroborating Madison's claims. Nobody knew about that note except him, Madison and Dillon.

But when Dillon and his men began to actively question all the young women in town, Brad would surely feel the heat. His hatred of Madison would know no bounds.

It was important that Flint stay vigilant in keeping the man away from Madison. He had no idea what Brad was really capable of. Murder? The thought chilled him to his aching bones.

All these things were on his mind the next evening when he and Madison left the cabin at nine. He had finally set up an after-hours doctor appointment for her with Clayton Rivers.

"Are you nervous?" he asked her once they were on their way.

"Not really. I'm relatively sure everything is going fine with the pregnancy. I've even felt the baby a couple of times. It's like a fluttering inside me." She wrapped her arms around her stomach and softly smiled.

"I'll still feel better once you and the baby are officially checked out by a doctor," he replied. He not only kept his gaze on the dark road ahead but also checked the rearview mirror often to make sure nobody came up on them out of the darkness with ill intent.

"And you're sure Dr. Rivers won't tell anyone about my condition?" she asked.

"Positive. Clayton is a good man and he didn't even question me on why we needed an appointment this late at night. I'm confident he won't tell anyone."

Flint didn't breathe easier until they were parked in the back lot of Dr. Rivers's office building. The building was dark except for a single light and Clayton opened the back door to let them in.

"Good evening," he greeted them.

He ushered them into his inner office and gestured them toward two chairs. "Maddy, I'm sorry about the stress you must be under right now, but tell me why you two are here." Flint hadn't gone into any detail when he'd arranged this after-hours appointment.

"I'm pregnant and I don't want anyone in town to know about it right now," Madison said. "I just don't want to be under more public scrutiny than I already am."

"Then I guess congratulations are in order for

the two of you?" Clayton raised one of his blond eyebrows.

"Oh…"

Before Madison could protest, Flint jumped in. "Yes, we're both very happy about the pregnancy. But with everything that's been going on she's been afraid to come in and get checked out."

Madison shot a grateful look to Flint and then gazed at the doctor. "I was hoping you could do a quick exam of me just to assure us that everything is progressing okay."

"I'd be more than happy to check you out." Dr. Rivers stood. "Let's all move into my examining room."

"Uh…if it's okay, I'll just wait here," Flint said. He breathed a sigh of relief as Dr. Rivers and Madison left the room. He had no idea what kind of an exam a doctor did on a pregnant woman. He didn't want to intrude on Madison's privacy.

As he waited, he hoped everything was all right with the pregnancy. He was vaguely surprised by how much he cared about the baby Madison carried. He almost felt like he was the real father.

It didn't take too long for the two of them to rejoin Flint in the office. Madison shot him a beautiful smile. "Dr. Rivers checked me out and everything is just fine."

Clayton nodded. "Mom is healthy and baby is developing normally."

"I told him not to tell me the sex of the baby," she said to Flint.

Clayton smiled at Flint. "She insisted she wants it to be a secret to both of you."

"When the baby makes an official appearance, then we'll know whether it's a boy or a girl," Madison replied.

"We really appreciate you meeting us after hours," Flint said as they left the office and headed for the back door.

"No problem," Clayton replied. "I understand your reasons for the late appointment. By the way, Flint, have you started that medication I prescribed for you yet?" he asked when Madison was almost out the door and presumably out of earshot.

"Uh, not yet. Things have been so crazy lately I haven't gotten around to it," Flint replied.

It wasn't until a few minutes later when they were in the truck and heading home that she brought it up, letting him know she had heard the doctor's question to him. "So what medicine are you supposed to be on that you aren't taking?" she asked.

"It's just some pain stuff for my broke-down bones," he replied. "I'll take it when I really feel like I need it. I'm just glad to know you and the baby are okay." He tried to deflect the conversation from him to her.

"Dr. Clayton told me he wants to see me again

in a month. I hope by then Brad is in jail and things go back to normal in my life...whatever normal is." She reached over and placed her hand on his thigh.

As always her touch fired a river of heat through him. She had no idea how tormented he was by his desire for her. "Thank you, Flint. Thank you not only for setting up this appointment but also for claiming the baby as your own and not telling the doctor that the baby is Brad's."

"I know how important it is to you that nobody knows that...although you do know the baby would be more evidence against Brad."

She pulled her hand back in her lap and released a deep sigh. "All the baby is is evidence of what Brad did to me. He'd twist it all around and say it was consensual sex and then his family would try to get the baby away from me."

She was silent for several long minutes as if she was deep in her own head. When he pulled up in front of the cabin she unfastened her seat belt and turned to look at him.

"I never meant for anyone to think that the baby is yours. That was the last thing I intended. I figured maybe I'd eventually tell anyone who asked that I had a brief affair with a man who was only in town a week or two and then he left Bitterroot."

"So it would be the old traveling salesman story?" he asked teasingly.

She laughed. "Something like that."

Her features were so beautiful in the light of the moon that drifted down and into the truck's window. "Madison, I'd be honored to claim your baby as my own and no matter what happens in the future I intend to be in his or her life until you find the special cowboy who will be with you forever."

His words were not only a reminder to her, but also to himself that he would not, could not, be that special cowboy.

A week had passed since Madison had seen the doctor, a long seven days where nothing had moved her case against Brad forward, and Flint had once again become distant.

She missed their easy conversations and shared laughter. She was now waiting for him to come inside so she could ask him why things had become strained between them. He'd gone outside first thing this morning to cut back some brush on the side of the cabin.

In fact, for the past week he'd found a variety of chores to keep him busy outside. It was like he was avoiding spending any time with her.

Was he tired of her? Exhausted by the drama? He certainly hadn't signed up for everything she'd brought into his life. He hadn't seen that in taking her in there would come a time where he'd have to wear his gun every time they left the cabin. He certainly hadn't seen a time coming when some of the people in town would shun him because of her.

There had been no more trouble since the shooting. Maybe Brad had realized that if anything happened to her, he would be the number one suspect. It was better for him to keep her alive and discredit her than to hurt her.

But she still was reluctant to move back to her trailer where she might be his victim of rape again. It was only by the grace of God that he hadn't gotten inside her trailer when he'd come there the second time.

She now made Flint's lunch and then went to the front door and called his name. He appeared from around the corner of the cabin. "Your lunch is ready," she said.

"Okay, I'll be right in."

She went back to the table and sat to wait for him. He came inside and cast her a brief smile. "I'm going to take a quick shower before I sit down to eat."

Fifteen minutes later he sat at the table across from her. He smelled of minty soap and a splash of his cologne and just the scent of him created a deep yearning for him.

She wanted to be in his arms again. She wanted him to kiss her until she was mindless, but for the past week more times than not he sat on the chair in the evenings to watch television. If he didn't even want to sit next to her, he certainly wasn't going to kiss her mindless.

"This looks good," he said as he picked up his fork.

"It's just a sandwich and some pasta salad," she replied.

"But it looks like a really good pasta salad," he said with a grin.

She smiled and focused on her plate. As they ate he talked a little bit about what he had left to do outside to get the landscaping around the cabin the way he wanted it.

"I also need to chop some wood and start getting a pile of good logs ready for when winter comes," he said.

"There's nothing better on a cold, wintry night than sitting in front of a roaring fire," she replied. "I love to listen to the snap and crackle of logs burning."

It was certainly easy for her to imagine being wrapped up in Flint's arms in front of a fire while it snowed outside. She listened to him talking about things he needed to get done and while he talked she wanted him. Oh, she wanted to touch his warm skin. She longed to be in his embrace and feeling his heartbeat against her own. She yearned for him to take her to bed again.

But at the moment the possibility of that happening was slim to none. She needed to have a conversation with him about the distance he'd shown her over the past week. She needed to know if she had overstayed her welcome. And if she had, she didn't know what she was going to do.

He helped her with the lunch cleanup. "Flint, would you sit on the sofa with me? I want to have a talk with you."

"Is everything okay?" he asked immediately.

"That's what I want to talk about," she replied.

"Okay." He moved to the sofa and she joined him there.

As she faced him she was suddenly nervous. Even now his forest-green eyes seemed to hold a slight distance she desperately wanted to banish. She wanted the warmth back in his gaze when he looked at her.

"Flint, I need you to be completely honest with me. Are you tired of my presence here?"

"Not at all," he replied instantly. "What would even make you think that?"

"You've been...distant for the past week. Something has changed between us and I need to know if I did or said anything wrong." Even just sitting next to him, her senses came alive in a way she'd never known before.

Not only was she captivated by his scent, but she could look at his handsome face for hours at a time, too. She would never forget the feel of his work-rough hands on her breasts, against her skin as he had stroked and caressed her.

When he'd claimed her baby as his own in the doctor's office, her love for him had flown off the charts. He was her dream man, but she was so afraid to tell him, so afraid that she would be rejected by him.

"Believe me, you have done nothing or said anything wrong," he replied.

"Then why have you been so distant with me? It's like you don't want to spend any time with me or talk to me." To her horror tears filled her eyes.

"Hey, don't get upset," he said and scooted closer to her. He reached out to swipe away the tears that escaped and fell to her cheeks.

"I'm sorry," she said with an embarrassed half laugh. She managed to get herself under control. "I just feel like something has changed and I don't know why. I... I need to understand what's going on."

He held her gaze for a long moment. "I have been distant with you," he admitted.

"But why?" she asked beseechingly.

His eyes darkened and flashed with a wild light that half stole her breath away. "Oh, woman, because you tempt me." His voice was a husky half growl. He leaned back from her and raked a hand through his still-dampened hair. "Sitting next to you on the sofa torments me. The scent of you makes my head dizzy with desire for you. And that's why I've been distant from you, because every minute we're together I want you."

"Oh, Flint." His words filled her with a sweet longing for him. She scooted closer and leaned into him. "I feel the same way about you, only my feelings for you make me want to be closer, not farther away from you."

She drew even nearer to him…so close she could feel his breath on her face; so close that her lips were mere inches from his. Their gazes locked for several long moments and then with a groan he covered her mouth with his.

Instantly, she was on fire and her heartbeat raced. She opened her mouth and their tongues swirled together in a heated dance. His arms circled around her, engulfing her in his scent and his sweet warmth.

"Madison," he groaned her name as his mouth left hers and blazed a trail down the side of her throat.

"I love the sound of my name when you say it," she replied as she leaned in as closely as she could get to him.

"Madison… Madison… Madison," he whispered along her jawline and then his lips crashed down on hers once again.

Although she wanted this moment of him kissing her with such desire to go on and on, what she didn't want was the two of them groping each other on the sofa like a couple of teenagers.

She pulled away from him. "Flint, I want you in bed," she said breathlessly. "Let's go into your bedroom." She stood and held out her hand to him.

He stared up at her, his eyes glazed with a wild hunger that thrilled her. He stood and took her hand and together they went into his bedroom. The minute they crossed the threshold he pulled her to him and kissed her once again.

Their bodies were so intimately close she could tell that he was fully aroused. She pressed her hips against him, her own desire rising so high she was half-mindless.

They tumbled to the bed and she grabbed the bottom of his T-shirt, wanting it off him so she could feel his beautiful, strong chest muscles. He finished the act, yanking his shirt off and tossing it to the nearby chair.

She ran her hands over his beautiful sculptured chest as he fumbled with the zipper at the back of her dress. His skin was so warm and inviting and at the moment all she wanted was to be naked with him.

He'd just managed to get her zipper down when a loud, firm knock sounded on the front door. He snapped up off the bed and drew several audible deep breaths before he grabbed his T-shirt and pulled it back on.

"I'll be right back," he said, his voice deeper than usual.

Madison remained on the bed for several long moments, hoping Flint would, indeed, come right back to the bedroom and they could resume what had been started.

Then she heard Dillon's deep voice and she knew there was no way Flint would return to finish what they had started. Reluctantly, she got up and reached behind her to zip her dress back up.

She drew in and released several deep breaths and then went into the living room where the two men were seated and visiting, obviously waiting for her to join them.

"Hi, Dillon," she said as she sat on the sofa next to Flint. She was interested in why Dillon was here, but she'd really much rather be in the bedroom making love with Flint.

"What's going on?" She looked at Dillon curiously.

"I wanted to let you know I've turned your case over to the District Attorney, but he still hasn't agreed to move forward on this."

"Is it possible Ainsworth money has played a part in the DA's reluctance?" Flint asked.

Dillon frowned. "I suppose anything is possible," he admitted slowly.

Madison sat up straighter on the sofa. "Have you

been conducting interviews around town? Have you been able to identify another victim?"

Dillon hesitated for a long moment and then shook his head. "My deputies and I have been conducting interviews with all the young women in town. There are two women who I think maybe something happened to them with Brad, but they insisted they had had no interactions with him."

"So what made you believe something might have happened?" Flint asked.

"They were both slightly evasive in their answers to me and I got several nonverbal tells that they were not telling me the truth. I also believe they were both afraid to even mention Brad's name."

"Who are they? Maybe I can talk to them and get them to be more forthcoming," Madison said. "Surely that would help my case immensely."

Dillon shook his head once again. "I'm sorry, but I have to respect their privacy."

"So it's still really just a he said-she said case and it's possible the DA has been bought off." Madison frowned. "There should be a way to catch Brad in the act of showing his monster face."

Her brain began to spin, trying to figure out a way to get additional evidence that would help her case. There had to be a way…there had to be something that could be done to catch a predator.

She'd watched shows on television about police setting up in a house to catch men who wanted sex with a minor. There had to be a way something like that could be done now. Her brain finally settled on a single truth.

What did a predator need to act?

He needed prey...

Chapter 12

"Absolutely not." Flint stared at Madison, wondering if the stress had finally sent her over the edge. She'd obviously lost her mind considering what she'd just offered Flint as a reasonable solution to the problem. Dillon had left only a few minutes ago and that was when Madison had sprung her hare-brained idea on him.

"Why not? It would be the perfect plan to catch him." She got up from the sofa and began to pace in front of Flint.

"Madison, there is no way in hell I want you using yourself as bait with that man," Flint said in protest. "He is dangerous and you could be seriously hurt."

"I know." She wrapped her arms around herself and for a moment her eyes appeared dark and haunted. "He *is* a dangerous predator and that's why he needs to be stopped here and now."

"Madison, for God's sake let the court take care of it." Flint was absolutely appalled by her idea.

"I don't trust the court to get it right. Who knows who the Ainsworths are paying off to keep their baby boy out of jail."

She started pacing once again. She walked back and forth in front of him and all he could think of was how small, how utterly defenseless, she appeared.

A rage surged up inside him at the thought of Brad hurting her...violating her. He wanted to kill the bastard, but he knew that wasn't really the answer, either.

"If this goes to court, Brad will paint me as a whore. He'll have everyone believing I'm the lowest of the low and he'll get other people to say the same things about me," she said.

"And I'll be glad to testify on your behalf. I'll tell people who you really are. I'll tell them that you're warm and giving and wonderful," he replied.

Her long hair rippled with the vehement shake of her head. "That's not enough. I appreciate that, but my idea is much better."

"Your idea is damned dangerous," he protested.

"Not if we all do it right." She walked around the coffee table and plopped back down next to him.

"Really think about it, Flint. All we have to do is spread the word around town that you're going to be out of town on a particular night. Then you and Dillon hide out in the woods. I know Brad probably believes that if I go away, this whole thing will go away. He'll come for me. You know he'll come for me."

"Look at yourself, Madison. You're shaking just talking about it." Flint pulled her close against his side, wanting to protect her from danger and now needing to somehow protect her from herself. "I'm sorry, Madison, but there is no way I can support a plan that in any way puts you in danger."

"But I wouldn't be," she protested and pulled away from him. "I want this to be over and done with, and this is an excellent plan and I intend to talk to Dillon about it first thing in the morning." She stood. "I hope you will support me in this... and now I'm going to take a little nap."

As she went into her bedroom Flint released a deep sigh. He had a feeling she'd decided to take a nap to escape his protests about her crazy plan.

He hoped that after she took her nap she would rethink her idea. There was no way he wanted her alone in the presence of Brad for a single minute, a single second.

However, he believed, like her, that if Brad thought

she was here all alone, then Brad would come after her. Flint believed that the man wouldn't be able to help himself.

Deciding that he wasn't going to entertain the idea any longer he turned on the television. He would have liked to go outside and do a little work, but he was hurting today. His hands were swollen and red and his hips burned with pain. It was definitely not a day to do any physical kind of work.

Except make love to Madison. His mind suddenly filled with what had been about to happen before Dillon had knocked on the door.

He and Madison had been about to make love again, and he was grateful that Dillon had interrupted them. While there was nothing he'd love more than to have Madison naked in his bed, it would have been a big mistake on his part.

But he admitted that Madison was definitely his weakness. When she leaned into him with a fire in her eyes, he found it hard to deny her, hard to not give in to his intense desire for her.

He had to be at a place to tell her goodbye when this was all over, and continuing to have any kind of a physical relationship with her would only make it more difficult.

Already the idea of not having her in his life created a dark pool of loneliness inside him. He couldn't believe how much he'd allowed her to get under his skin, into the very center of his heart.

He'd thought it was bad when big Cass had been killed by a large tree branch during a tornado, but that loss couldn't rival the loss in his life when Madison moved on.

And the idea of her using herself as bait to catch Brad absolutely terrified him. He could never condone any situation that put her life in any kind of risk.

Despite his protests to the contrary for the remainder of the night, he found himself the next morning sitting on the sofa and facing Dillon as Madison told the lawman her plan.

"Tell her it's a crazy plan, Dillon," he said once Madison had laid out her thoughts.

Dillon frowned and looked at Madison for a long moment. "Maybe crazy like a fox," he replied slowly. "Do you really think Brad would come after you if he thought you were alone here?"

"Without a doubt," she replied. "He'd come after me in a hot minute." Once again she had that stunning strength shining in her beautiful eyes.

"Dillon, the man already tried to kill her once by shooting at her. Surely you aren't really considering this," Flint exclaimed. "It's a crazy idea that shouldn't be considered for a minute."

Dillon turned his gaze to him. "But I've got to admit that I am considering Madison's plan. Let's be honest here, as she said, this kind of case can go either way and we all know that Brad and his family have friends in high places."

"All the more reason to do things my way," Madison replied firmly. "I want this over and done. It haunts me every night that he's out there with the capability of preying on another innocent victim. I want him off the streets sooner rather than later and this is a plan that will definitely get him arrested and off the streets."

She looked at Flint and then back at Dillon. "At this point what have we got to lose? It would just require a few hours of certain people's time and some help with technology. I feel confident that it could work."

"It's the *could* in your sentence that bothers me," Flint said.

"Okay, then I'm confident that it will work," she amended.

"Then maybe we should move forward with your plan," Dillon said after a long pause. "How about we set it up for Friday night? That will give you a couple of days to get the word out that Flint will be gone for the night."

"Does anyone care that I think this is a horrible idea?" Flint interjected.

Madison looked at him for a long moment, her eyes filled with a softness that created a thickness of emotion in his throat.

"Flint, I know you're worried about me, but this

is something I really need to do for myself. Please, Flint, I need your support in this."

Her eyes begged him and he was helpless to tell her he wouldn't support her. "Okay," he finally relented.

Like the old country song said, she was definitely his strongest weakness and he knew if this worked, then it was the beginning of goodbye for them.

Madison woke earlier than usual on Friday morning, nerves already beginning to jump in her veins. Tonight she would put herself out there for Brad to come after.

She snuggled deeper into the mattress. She'd be lying if she said she wasn't scared to death about the coming night. But she knew Flint and Dillon and two of Dillon's men would be hiding in the woods. Dillon was coming over in a couple of hours to wire her so that everything that transpired inside the cabin he would be able to hear outside.

Of course if Brad tried to rip her clothes off, then he'd find the wire, but Flint and the others would be inside long before that happened.

All she needed to do was get Brad to confess what he had done to her months before. Dillon would hear the confession and it would be part of the criminal prosecution. And, hopefully, that would be enough for Brad to be arrested and kept off the streets of Bitterroot. No other woman would be subjected to knowing the brutality of his fists, and no other woman would ever know what it was like to be sexually violated by him.

Her thoughts shifted from the night's activities to Flint. She'd seen the fear in his eyes when she'd been talking to Dillon to set this all up. She'd seen fear...and something else.

Love.

She could swear that was what she'd seen shimmering in the very depths of his eyes. It had been there for only a single, shining moment and then had been gone. But she'd seen it and embraced it and when this was all over she was going to tell him just how much she was in love with him.

She closed her eyes and imagined for a moment that she was Flint's wife. He would be in the delivery room when she had her baby...their baby. Oh, she wanted that to be a reality.

They would share the joy of the birth of her baby, and their life together would be filled with laughter and love. They'd snuggle together during the winters and enjoy the fire in the fireplace.

In the spring they'd plant flowers around the front of the cabin, flowers that would smell sweet and bloom in beautiful colors that reflected the beauty of their life together. She could envision it all so perfectly.

However, she couldn't claim that wonderful life

for herself until this horror story about Brad was over and done with forever. With this thought in mind, she rolled over and up out of bed.

The scent of coffee filled the air, letting her know that even though it was early, Flint was already up. She went directly into the bathroom and took a quick shower, then returned to her room to dress.

What did you wear to catch a predator? What did you wear to have a wire on? Unfortunately, she could no longer get into any of her jeans so her choices now were very limited.

She finally pulled on one of her sundresses that had sleeves and set her blue sweater on the bed to pull over it. At least with the sweater she should be able to hide whatever wire Dillon had her wear.

Her nerves settled a bit when she walked into the kitchen and saw Flint. He might be worried about the plan for the night, but she knew he would do everything in his power to keep her safe.

"Good morning," she said as she went to the cabinet for a cup.

"Back at you," he replied. "You're up early."

She put a cup of water in the microwave and then grabbed a tea bag. "Apparently, I got all my sleep out. But I did go to bed early last night."

They didn't speak again until she was seated across from him with her cup of tea. "Are you scared?" he asked.

"I'd be a fool not to be a little bit afraid, but I can't imagine what could go wrong." She stirred a spoonful of sugar into her tea.

"What if for some reason the mic doesn't work? What if Dillon doesn't hear when you're in trouble?" Flint's gaze searched her face as if memorizing it for the last time.

"Trust me. I won't need to wear a wire for you all to hear me if I'm in trouble. I can scream really, really loud." She took a sip of her tea.

"But what if he has his hand over your mouth?"

She slammed her cup down to the table. "What are you trying to do, Flint? Scare the hell out of me?"

His face flushed with color. "Sorry." He stared down into his coffee mug for a long moment and then looked back at her once again. "I guess I'm the one who is scared. I'm terrified for you, Madison."

She reached across the table and covered his hand with hers. "It's a good plan, Flint. More important, it's a safe plan." She pulled back her hand. "I trust you and Dillon and whoever comes with Dillon."

"I know, I know." He released a deep sigh. "I'll just feel better once this night is over and Brad is behind bars."

She smiled at him. "That makes two of us. Now, let's talk about something more pleasant."

"Like what?"

"I've been thinking that I'd love for you to help me come up with names for the baby."

"But we don't even know if it's a boy or a girl."

"And I've given it a lot of thought and I still don't want to know the sex before the birth, so we need to come up with the perfect boy and girl name."

"Hmm, that's a tall order. Do you have any ideas at all?"

"None, although it might be nice if it's a little girl to call her Abigail. That was my mother's name."

"Abigail is a pretty name," he replied.

What she'd love to do was name her son Flint Jr. in honor of the kind and generous man who had taken her in. He was the man who had saved her life…the man she loved deeply. But she had no place to ask him to give his name to the baby she carried. She had no right to ask him for anything more than he'd already given to her.

"And I'm assuming you don't want to name a boy after your father," he said.

"Goodness, no." She frowned as she thought of the man she had lived with for the first eighteen years of her life. He had been nothing more than a sperm donor who had reluctantly done his job. They had lived in the same space and he had raised her with verbal abuse and neglect.

"I've never given much thought to baby names before," Flint said, pulling her from her dark thoughts. "I'll have to think on it a bit."

"While you think on it, I'm going to make us some breakfast. How does a little bacon and some pancakes sound?"

"Sounds great to me," he said agreeably.

As she worked on fixing breakfast, the sizzle of the bacon cooking mirrored the sizzle of nerves in her veins as she contemplated the night.

Although she was one hundred percent certain that she would be safe, it was only natural that she be nervous. Facing Brad again would be incredibly difficult, but she was up to the task if it meant saving future victims.

"I don't hear any name suggestions falling from your lips," she said after a few minutes of silence. "Didn't you ever fantasize what you would name your children?"

"No, I never fantasized about having children."

She turned away from the pancake griddle to look at him. "Why is that? Didn't you ever think about having a family for yourself?"

"Never."

"But why?" She gazed at him curiously.

He shrugged. "It was just something I never saw for myself. I've never been that comfortable talking to women, let alone dating them."

"So what am I?" she replied with a touch of humor.

He grinned at her. "You're definitely all woman. I've actually been surprised by how easy I find it to talk to you, but that doesn't mean I've changed my mind about the path I've chosen for myself. It's a solitary path."

"Sounds like a lonely path to me." She turned around and then muttered a curse. Damn, she'd burned the first batch of pancakes.

Once they had the pancakes in front of them he asked her about her mother. "You never talk about her. Do you have any memories of her?" he asked.

"Not a whole lot, but some." She took a sip of her tea and then smiled as some of those memories fluttered through her.

"I remember the smell of her, a scent of lilacs and vanilla. I also remember the sound of her laughter. She was always smiling and finding funny things to laugh about. She found such joy in living. We had this special saying. I'd tell her I loved her and she'd tell me she loved me more. We'd argue about which one of us loved more."

Her smile faltered. "I never knew how sick she was. She hid it from me. Even when she lost her hair from the chemo treatments, she made jokes about it. And then she was just gone."

Flint drew her from her memories by covering her hand with the warmth of his. "She sounds like she was truly a beautiful woman."

"She was."

"And I think she'd be so proud of her daughter."

"Thank you, Flint," she replied. "No matter what

the circumstance, you always seem to know what to say."

"I always just speak what I see is the truth," he replied.

As usual, when he touched her in any way she wanted him. Although it was just his hand covering hers at the moment, she wished he would sweep her up in his arms and kiss her.

Instead, they finished breakfast and then cleaned up the dishes. Madison had a feeling this was going to be one of the longest days of her life.

Flint went into his bedroom and grabbed a duffel bag, which he placed by the front door for the pretend trip he would take later that evening. The plan was for him to drive to the Holiday Ranch where Mac would then take his truck and drive it out of town.

Meanwhile, Jerod would drop Flint back at the mouth of the lane to the cabin after dark. And that was when Dillon and his men would also move into their positions hiding in the woods and waiting for the action to begin.

"Are you sure you don't want to call this off?" Flint asked once he'd placed his duffel bag by the door.

"No way," she immediately replied. "I just can't wait for it all to be over with. I want to see that man in handcuffs and Dillon hauling him out of the cabin and out of our lives forever."

"I sure as hell hope that's exactly what happens," Flint replied fervently.

For the next several hours they took turns pacing the floor and waiting for the hours of the day to tick down. They ate lunch and then paced some more.

"We're wearing out your floors," she joked as she sat on the sofa and watched him pacing back and forth in front of the coffee table.

"I can't help it. I don't know about you, but as it gets later in the day I get more nervous about the night to come," he replied.

"Trust me. I feel the same way," she replied. She'd been trying to downplay just how nervous she was getting for Flint's sake. But the truth was she was getting so nervous she felt like screaming.

It was three o'clock when Dillon came by to wire Madison. "Thank God for the advancement of technology," he said as he affixed a tiny wireless microphone into the collar of her blue sweater.

"It's so small," Madison said worriedly.

"It might be small, but it's mighty," Dillon replied. "It's definitely strong enough to pick up all the sounds in the room and those sounds will be audible to me in an earpiece. You don't need to do anything but keep your sweater in the living room where you'll face Brad if all goes as planned and he actually shows up here."

Dillon turned to look at Flint. "We'll all plan on being in our positions about nine tonight. I checked the local forecast and there are some clouds moving in so it should be dark by then. You should plan on leaving here around eight-thirty."

"But that means she'll be alone here between eight-thirty and nine," Flint protested.

"Brad won't show up that early," Madison replied. "He'll come in the dead of night, hoping to catch me sleeping and unprepared."

"Maybe I should leave my gun with you." Once again the deep concern was in Flint's eyes.

She shook her head. "No, I don't want to have a gun. I don't know how to shoot and I don't want him getting it away and using it on me. I'm comfortable with the plan the way it stands. As long as you all ride to my rescue if I scream, I'm good."

"You know that's going to happen," Flint assured her.

Once Dillon left to head back into town, Flint and Madison had nothing to do but wait until it was time for Flint to leave the cabin.

Madison curled up on the sofa to read even as Flint continued to pace the floors. He was obviously far more nervous than she was. Her nerves had settled the minute Dillon had put the mic on her.

"Flint, for goodness' sake come sit down," she said after about fifteen minutes. "Your pacing is driving me crazy."

He moved to the sofa and sat down next to her.

He released one of his deep sighs. "I don't want to leave you here alone tonight."

"I know, but this has to be done. You'll be out there in the woods and I know the minute you think I'm in danger you'll charge in here with guns blazing."

"You can bet on that," he replied fervently.

It was her turn to deeply sigh. "If all goes as planned tonight, then tomorrow when I wake up I'll feel freer than I have since the night of the initial attack. I can't wait to feel that again."

"I have a feeling if all goes well there will be a lot of young women silently thanking you for your courage tomorrow."

She released a dry laugh. "I'm not courageous. I'm in survival mode. I might be doing this for other victims, but ultimately I'm doing it to help myself."

"I'll just be glad when this is all over."

Flint repeated those same words at eight-thirty that evening when she walked him to the front door. He had his empty duffel bag in hand and a deep reluctance in his eyes as he gazed at her.

"It's going to be fine, Flint," she said softly.

"It has to be fine," he replied.

"You're already supposed to be out of here," she chided him.

"I know. I'm going." He suddenly dropped his bag to the floor and pulled her into his arms. Before she could even catch her breath he was kissing her long and hard.

It was a kiss that warmed her to her toes, a kiss not just of passion, but also of something else… something soft and wonderful. Her love for him bubbled up inside her. She wanted to tell him just how much she loved him but now was not the time or the place. He had to leave and she couldn't stop him and screw up the plan by a sudden confession of her deepest emotions.

He finally pulled his lips from hers and released her. Without saying another word he turned and walked out the door. She closed and locked up behind him and then leaned with her back against the door.

She closed her eyes and raised her fingers to her lips where the imprint of his mouth still burned. There was no question in her mind…there had been love in his kiss.

However, she couldn't think about that right now. She had things to do before Brad showed up. She opened her eyes and pushed off the door. She went directly into the kitchen and grabbed a couple of Flint's shiny, sharp knives from the drawer.

Shoving them in various places under the sofa cushions, she then sat to await Brad's appearance. She trusted the men outside, but she felt better with the knife or three hidden away just in case she needed it. She just hoped Brad didn't find any of them before she needed one.

She had two reasons to live through the night. The first reason was the baby growing inside her, and the second was so she'd get a chance to tell Flint how very much she loved him. Now, all she had to do was survive this night and a date with a monster.

Chapter 13

Flint walked through the dark woods, his heart pounding like a million wild horse hooves. He headed to the place at the mouth of the lane where Dillon and his men would be. As he walked, his mind was filled with thoughts of the woman he loved, the woman he would never really have.

The kiss they had shared just before he'd left the cabin was the last one they would ever have, although he would cherish the memories of each and every kiss they'd had since the moment he'd found her in the barn.

Still, he would give his life to keep her safe through this night. When he thought of her facing

Brad all alone, his heart once again raced and he could scarcely catch his breath.

He arrived at the place where he was to meet Dillon. Apparently, the lawman hadn't arrived yet. Nothing appeared amiss, but Flint imagined he could smell the scent of something evil coming closer.

It was too bad evil people didn't have a distinctive smell to them. It would certainly make them easier to identify. It sickened him when he thought about how often Brad had shaken his hand, how quick the man was to smile in a way that made him appear nonthreatening and wholesome.

Nobody, absolutely nobody in the entire town would have thought Brad to be so evil. Nobody except the women who had been his victims. He prayed that tonight there was no way Madison would be his victim again.

Some of his anxiety lowered when Dillon, along with officers Juan Ramirez and Ben Taylor, found him. Somebody had apparently dropped them off for Flint hadn't seen or heard any cars anywhere near the place.

He greeted the men in a mere whisper. If it hadn't been for a cell phone light from Dillon's phone, he wouldn't have been able to see them in the darkness. "Have you tried out the mic to see if it's working?" he asked Dillon.

The lawman raised his hand to an earbud in his

ear. "Madison and I just tested it and it's working fine. Right now she's singing 'Little Boots.'"

Flint couldn't help the small smile in his heart. The song was currently popular on the country-western charts and was about a couple shopping for little cowboy boots for their soon-to-be-born son. She'd been humming it or singing it for the past week or so.

"This may be a long night," Dillon said.

"However long it takes, right?" Flint replied. "It's time to get this bastard off the streets."

With that, Dillon told each of them where to station themselves for the night to come. He didn't have to tell them to stay undercover and keep quiet. They all understood that potentially Madison's life could be on the line. There was absolutely no room for mistakes.

Flint took his position on the left side of the house. Although the woods were dark and dense, the moonlight overhead was bright and the cabin was bathed in the silvery illumination.

What was Madison doing as she waited for the devil to show up at the door? Her fear had to be tremendous. As great as his was, hers would be tenfold. She was the one with her life on the line.

He wished he were inside the cabin with her right now, holding her closely...protectively. He wished he were close to her to feel her body heat, to smell her sweet scent and feel her heart beating next to his.

He wanted to be her dragon slayer. He touched the butt of his gun. He'd like to take Brad out before the man ever reached the cabin's front door. As far as he was concerned Brad was a guilty man the minute he stepped foot on this property.

But he knew it was important to Madison for her to feel as if she'd slayed her own dragon with just a little bit of help from the rest of them.

And if she was successful tonight, if Brad really did show up here, then it would be goodbye for Flint and Madison. He'd already talked to the garage and arranged to pay for her car repairs. It would be ready for her first thing in the morning.

With Brad in jail there would be nothing holding her back from reclaiming her former life...a life without Flint. He had a feeling he was going to break her heart, as he now realized that casting her back into her own life would break his own.

But it would be selfish of him to keep her in his life. She needed her freedom to chase the dream she wanted. He couldn't, he would never, be her dream.

He hoped Brad showed up tonight. Flint needed this over as much as she needed it. It was growing more and more difficult for him to be around her and not make love with her once again. It was growing more and more difficult for him not to tell her that he was in love with her.

He stared at the cabin's front door as the minutes ticked by with agonizing slowness. Thoughts of Madison continued to flood his mind. Their first kiss…her charming laughter…making love to her…finding her in the hay…it all played in his mind like clips from a movie.

Minutes moved into an hour, then another hour. As it got later and later, Flint's tension rose. The muscles in his belly and chest tightened. His heartbeat quickened and he was acutely aware of the sounds around him.

Night bugs clicked and whirred and occasionally the brush surrounding him rustled with little nocturnal creatures that lived in the woods.

More time passed and Flint began to wonder if Brad was going to show up. Would he be bold enough to just drive in or would he sneak in on foot like a thief in the night?

Flint had a feeling if he came at all, he would come in quietly. Hopefully, he wouldn't see or stumble over any of the men lying in wait for him.

God, he just wanted this night over and he wanted Madison to be safe and sound. This plan had to work with Brad taking the bait and everything going as planned.

Flint changed positions and began to wonder if all this was for nothing. His knees and hips had begun to burn painfully, but he tried to ignore the agony and remain vigilant. His gaze hadn't wavered from the cabin's front door.

A soft rustling noise sounded behind him and suddenly something hard crashed into the back of his head. Pain slashed into him as stars flashed in his vision.

Madison. Her name screamed in his head just before utter darkness claimed him.

There had been four of them hiding in the woods. And all four had been taken out thanks to Brad's friends. They were all unconscious and bound. The chief of police and Flint must have believed he was some kind of fool. He'd known this was a setup from the get-go. There was no way Flint McCay would travel out of town and leave his precious Madison vulnerable.

The friends who had helped him would alibi each other for tonight and Brad's girlfriend would alibi him. He'd known it was a seteup, but that didn't mean he wasn't going to take advantage of the situation.

Any threat had now been neutralized and all that was left was dealing with the stupid bitch who was trying to destroy his life. Right now there were no witnesses and after he dealt with Madison and left here there would still be no witnesses.

Madison wouldn't live through this night. In fact, she wouldn't live through the next thirty minutes. He approached the cabin door, already excited by what he was going to do to the woman inside.

Boldly, he knocked on the front door. There was no way Madison was peacefully sleeping inside. She'd be expecting him. Sure enough, the door crept open.

Her big blue eyes widened as if she was surprised to see him and before she pretended to slam the door, he shoved it open. "Honey, I'm home," he said gleefully.

For the past several hours Madison had wanted to scream with the nerves that twisted her stomach and kept her half-breathless.

She'd paced and she'd sang in an effort to keep her nerves under control. She'd checked the knives beneath the sofa cushions at least a dozen times as she'd waited for Brad to arrive.

When the knock had fallen on the door, she'd fought the survival instinct that had told her not to answer. But she had answered and now she was facing her monster.

She backed away from him. "What are you doing here, Brad? Are you here to beat me up and rape me again?"

"Definitely, and that will only be the beginning." His eyes gleamed with a sickness she remembered all too well. "I liked beating you up and I definitely enjoyed raping you so much I'm now here for seconds."

Her heartbeat became a rush in her ears. She'd thought she was strong enough to face him, but as she continued to back away from him her shaky legs threatened to cast her to the floor.

She prayed for the door to burst open and Flint and the others to come to her rescue. Hadn't he already confessed to the previous crime? Hadn't she already gotten enough from him?

He laughed. "I see you looking at the front door. Waiting for your boyfriend or maybe Dillon to come in to help you? I'm sorry, but they weren't invited to this party of two and in any case, they're all unconscious and tied up right now." He laughed once again, the maniacal sound echoing in the room.

Still, his words disturbed her far more than his laughter. Unconscious? Tied up? "Wha...what did you do to them?" Oh, God, was he lying to her? Had he killed them all?

"Don't worry about it. Did you really think I wouldn't know this was a setup? Did you really believe I was so stupid? All you really have to do is know that they aren't coming to your rescue. Nobody is riding to your rescue. It's just you and me, baby, and we're going to have some fun."

Flint... Dillon? Nobody was going to rush in to save her from this man? Terror gripped her heart, her very soul. With a gasp, she ran for the bedroom. She slammed the door and for the first time realized the door didn't have a lock on it.

In desperation, she pressed her back against it and dug her heels into the carpeting. Damn, she should have run into Flint's bedroom where at least there was a phone. In here she had no way to summon any help and she knew the cabin was isolated enough there would be nobody to hear her screams. But she did scream as Brad twisted the doorknob and shoved against the door.

He was going to get in and then what? What had he done to Flint and the others? She'd die if anything horrible had happened to Flint. This thought brought a bubble of hysterical laughter to her lips. What was she thinking? She was going to die tonight anyway.

The hysterical laughter turned into another scream as Brad once again pressed to get inside the room. His strength was far greater than hers and he managed to get his head and shoulders into the door. "Come on, Madison, let's have some fun together. Don't you remember how much fun we had last time?"

She desperately tried to keep him out, but as she realized she couldn't, she released her fragile grasp on the door and instead scrambled to the opposite side of the bed.

Brad stepped into the room and grinned at her.

"Just give in, Madison. Did you really think I was going to allow you to ruin my name? My life?"

"Just leave now and I'll take it all back. I'll tell Dillon I lied about you, that I was mad because you didn't want to go out with me. I swear, Brad, I'll do that if you just turn around and walk out the door."

"It's a little too late for that, Madison. The only way to make things right is if you go away." He faced her from across the bed.

"Then I'll leave town. I'll even leave the state. I promise you I'll pack up and be gone first thing in the morning." She would promise him anything right now to get him out of the cabin. "Please, Brad, just leave now."

"Please, Brad," he mimicked her. "Say it again, Maddy. I love it when you beg."

"I swear to you I'll recant and leave town if you just leave me alone," she exclaimed. She was half-breathless with her fear of him. Her heart felt as if it was going to beat right out of her chest.

"I told you. It's just too late for any of that," he said. His eyes gleamed once again and he grinned widely. "Besides, I've missed you." He leaped over the bed toward her, but his foot somehow tangled in the bed skirt and he fell to the side.

She ran past him, raced out of the bedroom and toward the front door. If she could just get outside, then she could hide in the woods until some sort of help could be summoned. She could hide until Brad gave up and left.

Before she could reach the front door he grabbed her by the ankle. As she fell to the floor she wrapped her arms around her belly to protect her baby.

The fall momentarily stunned her. Her baby. The words screamed in her head. Oh, God, if Brad managed to kill her tonight, he would also assure the death of the innocent life that grew inside her.

Brad still had her ankle and he began to drag her closer to him. She used her other foot against him. She kicked and twisted to free herself from his grip.

Finally, her foot connected and slammed him in the side of the face. He laughed even as she slipped free of his hold.

A sob rose up inside her as she quickly scrambled to her feet. Brad laughed again as if this all was some kind of a playful game they played. Only in this game the loser died.

He quickly moved so he stood between her and the front door. "Scream again, Madison. It excites me so much when you scream."

One of the knives hidden beneath the sofa cushion was only a foot or so away from where she stood, but she was afraid to grab it in her current breathless state.

When she did grab it she had to make sure she was strong enough to use it without him taking it away from her. Now wasn't the time, but she prayed the time would come and she could use the knife effectively against him.

And if she couldn't do that, and if she couldn't somehow run away from him, then tonight she would die.

Chapter 14

Consciousness came to Flint with an agonizing pain in the back of his head. For a moment he couldn't make sense of where he was or what was going on.

Darkness surrounded him and he was lying on his side. What had happened? Why did his head hurt so badly? As he tried to raise his hand to touch the painful place in his head, he realized he couldn't. His hands were bound behind his back.

Panic clawed inside him as everything came into focus. Madison! Her name shrieked in his head. What was going on? How long had he been out? And where were Dillon and the other men?

He managed to maneuver himself to his knees and worked at trying to free his hands from whatever bound them. "Dillon!" He cried out as loud as he could. What in the hell was going on? "Dillon?" There was no reply.

Every nerve in his body electrified. He struggled to his feet as his hands twisted and turned in an effort to get free. He stumbled several steps toward the cabin, all the while calling out to Dillon and the other men.

Even if he managed to get inside, there wasn't much he could do with his hands tied behind his back. He yanked his wrists and gasped as he finally felt them give just a little bit. He twisted and pulled more frantically despite the pain he was causing himself.

"Flint?" Dillon's voice came from somewhere on Flint's right.

"Yeah, yeah, I'm over here," Flint replied.

He heard Dillon stumbling through the woods toward him. At the same time Flint managed to free one of his hands, and then the other.

Dillon appeared out of the darkness in front of him. His hands were tied behind his back, as well. "What the hell happened?" Flint asked as he worked on the ropes that bound Dillon's hands.

"Somebody obviously got the jump on us," Dillon replied.

He'd just managed to free Dillon when Madison screamed. The cry echoed off the trees and iced Flint's blood.

Thankfully, both men still had their weapons. They drew them and then raced for the cabin. Before they reached the front door, not only did Madison scream once again, but Brad roared.

How long had she been inside alone with Brad? What had happened to her while Flint and Dillon and the others had been unable to respond?

Thank goodness the door was open, otherwise Flint would have gone through the wood to get to her. He ran through the door with Dillon at his heels and both men froze.

Madison sat on the floor, her dress torn and tears trekking down her cheeks. Brad was also on the floor some distance away from her with a knife protruding from his thigh.

"Dillon, arrest this bitch," Brad yelled. "Look what she did to me. Arrest her!"

Flint raced to Madison's side and helped her up off the floor. "Oh, God, Madison, are you okay?" He raked his gaze over her from head to toe, grateful not to see any discernible wounds.

She threw her arms around his neck and clung to him. Her entire body trembled and all he wanted to do was take away any negative emotions that might be rushing through her.

"I stabbed him, Flint. I got the knife and I

stabbed him," she said. There was a hint of pride in her voice. "I got him. I got him all by myself."

"Did you hear her? She admitted it. Arrest her and get an ambulance out here," Brad exclaimed as he managed to make it to his feet. Flint knew the knife wound probably hurt like hell, but it was obvious it hadn't nicked any artery. In fact, it had almost stopped bleeding.

"I'm going to make an arrest, but I won't be arresting her," Dillon replied as he yanked Brad's arms behind him. "Brad Ainsworth, you're under arrest for rape and attempted murder to name just a few charges."

"I didn't rape her," Brad replied angrily. "Okay, I'll admit we had a consensual relationship. That bitch wanted me. She told me Flint was going to be out of town tonight and she invited me over. Look at her. She's pregnant and it's my baby."

Flint's blood boiled over. He couldn't stand even looking at the man. He stepped away from Madison and before Dillon could stop him he punched Brad in the jaw. Brad yelped. "That's my baby, you sick bastard," Flint said. "She was pregnant with my child before you raped her."

At that moment Juan and Ben came into the cabin. Ben used Flint's phone to call for an ambulance and backup while Flint, unable to listen to or look at Brad again, took Madison into her bedroom.

He pulled her down to sit by his side. "Are you sure you aren't hurt?" He took her hands in his.

"I'm okay. He's going to jail now, isn't he?" Her beautiful eyes gazed into his.

"He's going to jail for a very long time," Flint replied. "It's over, Madison. It's finally over and you can have your life back."

She leaned against him. "Right now all I want to do is stay in here until he's gone and then I want to sleep."

The ambulance finally arrived and as they remained in her room he told her about all of them being hit over the head and tied up.

"I was so afraid he'd killed you all," she said. "Are you sure you're okay?"

"I'm perfectly fine now that I know that you're okay," he replied.

Flint knew in the coming days Dillon would be looking for accomplices. There was no way Brad had taken them all out by himself. He had to have had help.

Dillon finally appeared in the doorway. "He's gone and now I need to take Madison down to the station to make an official statement."

"Can't it wait until tomorrow? She's exhausted," Flint replied.

"No, it's okay. I'd just as soon get all this behind me as soon as possible." She stood and held out her hand to Flint. "But could you please come with me?"

"Absolutely."

As they rode in the back of Dillon's patrol car, Flint's love for her nearly choked him. This night could have ended so much differently. If she hadn't hidden the knife…if Brad had managed to get it away from her…if…if…

The *ifs* haunted him. However, her strength awed him. She'd slayed her own dragon and he hoped in doing so she found a peace she'd been lacking since the original attack.

When they reached the police station Dillon ushered them into his private office and Madison began telling him what had occurred while she'd been alone with Brad.

As Flint listened to her, he was almost grateful Brad was now in the custody of the law; otherwise, Flint would have beaten the man to a pulp.

"I guess you didn't hear him confess to beating and raping me," she said to Dillon. "So the mic wasn't worth anything."

"On the contrary, I might not have heard it with my own ears, but…" He reached into his pocket and pulled out a miniature recorder. "Anything that was said in that cabin was captured on tape. Don't worry, Madison. We have him and no amount of his parents' money or status is going to get him out of this."

"You were amazing in doing this," Flint said to her softly. She squeezed his hand and smiled and then continued to tell Dillon how she managed to get the knife out from beneath the sofa cushion and stab Brad in the leg.

Her eyes flashed for a minute. "I would have liked to stab him in his black heart, but at least by stabbing him in the leg I stopped him from coming after me. I was going to get up and run outside and hide in the woods until somebody came to help me."

Flint squeezed her hand. "I'm so damned sorry I wasn't there when you needed me."

"But you were…and you are." She squeezed his hand back.

In that moment he could scarcely keep his love for her inside him. He wanted to fall to his knees in front of her and tell her how very much he loved her and the baby that grew inside her.

He wanted to take her up and into his arms and kiss her until the end of the world. Instead, he bit the inside of his mouth to keep his love words inside him.

Tomorrow he would be telling her goodbye and that was the right thing to do. He couldn't be selfish enough to proclaim his love for her knowing that he could never be her dream man.

An overwhelming weight settled on his shoulders as they returned to the patrol car for Dillon to take them home. For whatever was left of this night, it would be the last night they spent together.

Dillon's crime scene men were finished in the cabin and they were finally all alone. "I'm so exhausted," she said as she collapsed on the sofa.

"Just think, tomorrow when you wake up you can claim your life back. You no longer have to think about leaving Bitterroot and I'll bet Sharon down at the grocery store will give you your job back."

"Before that can happen I feel like I need to sleep for about the next twenty-four hours."

"Then that's what you should do," he replied.

She got up from the sofa, her weariness evident in the forward slump of her shoulders. She gazed up at him.

"Flint, would you please sleep with me tonight?" Her eyes held a silent appeal.

He wanted to be strong and tell her it wasn't a good idea. It was important that they gain some distance from each other. But as he thought of everything she'd been through, he couldn't tell her no. Surely there would be no harm in them sharing his bed for whatever was left of the night.

Minutes later they were in her bed and she immediately moved into his arms. He was only grateful that she wore a nightgown and he had on his boxers.

Her head found the hollow of his neck and her

breathing was a soft whisper against the underneath of his chin. He drew in the sweet, floral scent of her and tried to memorize how her body fit against his. She fell asleep almost immediately, obviously exhausted by what she'd been through, but it took him much longer to finally drift off.

He would never again hold her in his arms. He would never taste the sweetness of her lips. He was already mourning her being gone from his life.

There would be no more laughter between them. He would never see the charming little wrinkle that danced across her forehead when she was deep in thought.

There were so many things he was going to miss when she left. He would miss the sound of her humming or singing, how her very presence filled the cabin with a warm energy. God, he hated the coming of tomorrow.

He finally drifted off asleep and awakened to sunshine whispering through the curtains. Madison was on the other side of the bed and was still sound asleep. He rolled out of bed and to his feet, grateful that his movements didn't awaken her.

He grabbed his jeans from the nearby chair and then padded into the bathroom. After a quick shower he went into the kitchen, made himself a cup of coffee and then sat at the table.

It was still early and he expected Madison to

sleep for several more hours and he would use that time to prepare himself to tell her goodbye.

When it got late enough he'd call Larry Wright at the car dealership and would see if somebody could bring Madison's car here. That way when she left here she'd have her car, and her trailer and a new life.

She'd be fine without him, and eventually… hopefully he'd be fine without her. He'd never expected to love her. When he'd found her in the hay and had offered her the cabin, he'd never dreamed that she would manage to get so deeply into his heart.

These feelings he had for her…he'd never experienced them before. He'd never had a woman share so much of herself with him, and he had certainly never before, with any other woman, shared himself like he had with Madison.

God, he wanted her. He wanted her in his life forever. He wished he could spend the rest of his life with her by his side. He ached with the desire to sleep with her every night, and build dreams with her during the days.

He wanted to help her raise her baby. He'd never dreamed he'd want to have his own family, and yet that was what Madison offered him and he hadn't known how badly he wanted it until now…when it was finally time to tell her goodbye.

He now dreaded her waking up. He knew he was

going to hurt her, but it had to be done. He had to love her enough to let her go.

By the time he finished his first cup of coffee it was late enough to call Larry. The arrangements were made to get Madison's car to the cabin around ten-thirty. He made himself another cup of coffee and then moved to the sofa and turned on the television with the volume soft enough it wouldn't bother Madison.

He imagined when the local news came on at noon Brad would be part of that report and the whole town would finally know what he had done not only to Madison, but potentially to other women, as well.

It would be a huge shock to many of the people in town who admired and liked Brad, people who hadn't known just how evil and sick he was. Everyone had just assumed he had a golden future ahead of him. Well, now he could have his future in prison.

Madison would be able to hold her head up high and he imagined going forward she would get lots of sympathy and support.

Now, all he had to do was wait for her to get up, and then he would tell her goodbye.

Madison awoke and slowly stretched beneath the sheet. She had slept without dreams and now felt completely rested. She opened her eyes to the sunshine drifting through the window. What time was it?

She rolled over and looked at the clock on the nightstand. Almost eleven. She knew it was late, but she hadn't realized it was that late.

Before she could pull herself out of bed the events of the night played in her head. Brad trying to attack her and almost succeeding. She'd known his intention had been to rape and kill her. But in the end she had won. And now she was free.

Free.

Her heart swelled in her chest. He could never, ever hurt her again. She could go about her life and never have to even think about Brad Ainsworth again.

And she wanted her life to be here with Flint. She'd known for some time that he was her dream man and now with the danger finally gone, they could enjoy a new life together.

With this thought in her mind, she got up and got dressed. Even her dresses were getting tight around her belly. But now she could go shopping for some maternity clothes.

She could go out to lunch with a friend without being afraid. She might be able to get her job back and work until she delivered the baby. She could do whatever she wanted and know Brad was gone forever.

Happiness raced through her as she left the bedroom and found Flint seated at the kitchen table. "Good morning," she said. "I can't believe I slept so late." She went to the cabinet to get a cup for her tea.

"You deserved it. It was a long night."

She made her drink and then sat across from him. "How are you feeling?" he asked.

She smiled. "Wonderful. How about you? Did you get enough sleep?"

"I got enough." He looked down into his coffee cup and then gazed at her once again. "I had your car fixed and it's now outside ready for you to go back to your trailer."

She looked at him in surprise. "But...but... I haven't earned enough money to fix the car. I still need to work for you to earn more money."

"Madison, you'll need the car when you leave here. Consider it a gift from me. Just say thank you and we'll call it even."

She continued to gaze at him. "I don't want to."

"Just say thank you," he repeated.

"Thank you."

It was just another act of kindness that dug him deeper into her heart. Now, with the danger of Brad gone, she felt free and eager to claim that love.

And suddenly she needed to tell Flint exactly how she felt about him. Her love for him filled her so much and she now needed to express it to him.

"You said I'll need the car when I leave here, but

what if I don't want to leave here?" She reached across the table and captured one of his hands with her. "What if I want to stay here forever?"

He winced and pulled his hand away from hers. "Madison, the danger is over and so it's time for you to go back to your life."

"But I want my life to be with you. Flint, I'm in love with you. I can't imagine ever loving a man like I do you."

Her heart trembled as she waited for his reply.

She'd hoped his eyes would light up at her words, that he'd laugh with joy and pull her up and into his arms. But that didn't happen.

Pain, rather than joy, pulled his features taut. "Madison, it's only natural that you'd think you were in love with me. After everything you've been through I'm sure with a little time you'll realize you've mistaken love for gratefulness."

"Flint, I am grateful to you for everything you've done for me, but that is completely separate from the love I have in my heart for you."

He drew an audible breath and released it slowly. He held her gaze for only a moment and then looked down at the table. "I'm sorry, Madison, but I don't love you."

"You're lying," she whispered.

"It's the truth. I'm sorry, Madison."

This time her heart trembled with an entirely different emotion. Why was he denying the love she knew he had for her? "I know you love me, Flint. A woman knows when a man loves her. Why are you lying to me?"

"I'm not." He got up from the table and moved into the living room, but she was right on his heels.

"Flint, please tell me what's going on right now." She'd had a hundred fears leading up to last night. She'd believed it was possible Brad would rape her again, that he would kill her. She'd thought she would never be believed in her allegations against him, but she'd never, ever imagined that Flint would deny her his love.

He sat on the sofa and stared out the window. She sank down next to him, tears welling up inside her and burning at her eyes. "Flint...please talk to me."

"There's nothing to talk about. I told you that this was a place just for me, that I had no intention of living...of loving anyone."

"You told me that before you really knew me, before we made love and lived and laughed together." The tears that had threatened now blurred her vision and spilled onto her cheeks. She swiped at them as she continued to stare at the man she loved.

"I love you, Flint, and I want to be with you forever. I want you to be the father of this baby and all of us to live together." Tears half choked her as she couldn't believe this was happening.

"Madison, please don't make this more difficult than it is. You got through the danger and now it's time you make your own way. I hope you eventually find the man who is right for you and can give you all your dreams."

He finally looked at her. His eyes were dark and shuttered against her. "You are that man, Flint," she said softly. "You are the man of my dreams, the wonderful cowboy I want by my side for the rest of my life."

"I can't be your cowboy," he exploded and jumped to his feet. "I can't be anybody's cowboy. I don't know what I'm going to be."

She frowned up at him. "What are you talking about?"

He raked a hand through his hair and stared at her for a long moment. "I've got rheumatoid arthritis, Madison. I can't be your dream man. I'm damaged goods."

"You aren't damaged." She slowly got to her feet. "Does this have something to do with the pills your doctor mentioned?"

He gave her a curt nod. "It's a drug to slow the progression."

"And are you taking it?"

He hesitated. "I haven't started it yet."

"Why not? And does rheumatoid arthritis stop you from loving me?" She took a step closer to him. "How about you start taking the medicine and we'll face whatever comes together?"

He closed his eyes for a long moment and then

gazed at her. "Don't you get it, Madison? I'm not going to spend my days riding the range or roping cattle. I'm not going to be a cowboy anymore."

"Oh, Flint. You couldn't stop being a cowboy if you wanted. A cowboy is someone who protects the weak. He's respectful and kind and honest. He values his friends and those he loves. You are forever a cowboy, Flint, and it doesn't matter what hat you wear or if you never climb on the back of a horse again. You are my forever cowboy, Flint. All you have to do is open up your heart and know that we belong together."

His eyes filled with tears. "I don't know what my future holds."

"Neither do I, but we'll be strong together. Oh, Flint…just love me."

"I do," he choked. He held up his arms toward her and she ran into his embrace.

"I love you, Madison, and I already love the baby." His lips took hers in a kiss that stole her breath away and filled her head with thoughts of lust-filled nights and days of laughter.

"I want you here with me for all my days and all of my nights," he said when the kiss finally ended. His eyes shone that wonderful green that invited her into the depths of his heart.

And that was exactly where she wanted to be.

Epilogue

The past four days had been a whirlwind of activity as Madison moved things from her trailer to the cabin. Flint's bookshelf now held an array of romance novels and she had an entire drawer in the bathroom dedicated to her makeup and personal items.

Female touches made the space look and feel more like home and he hadn't even minded when she'd taken over the spare room closet and then had encroached on his in the master bedroom.

There were moments when he needed to pinch himself to believe that this was all real, that she knew all his flaws and still wanted to be with him. And there were moments when he'd catch her gaze on him and see her love for him shining in those beautiful blue depths and it would steal his breath away.

They had shared a discussion about how to transform the second bedroom into a nursery and she'd made an appointment for next week to meet with Ellie Miller, a local psychologist who hopefully would be able to help Madison with the trauma she'd suffered at Brad's hands.

The plan at the moment was when she was ready to leave, they were heading into town to buy her some maternity clothes and then later they would go out to dinner at the café.

It would be the first time they'd been out socially since Brad's arrest, and he suspected this would be a much different experience than what they had shared at the café before.

She came out of the bedroom clad in a pink flowered dress and with her hair falling soft and shiny beneath her shoulders. She placed her hands on her stomach. "It's a good thing I'm buying some new maternity clothes today. Everything is getting too tight on me."

"You still look beautiful," Flint said, earning him her warm smile.

"Let's get out of here before your sweet talk seduces me right into your bed."

He laughed and together they left the cabin. Two hours later they got back into his truck to head to the café. She was now clad in a pair of maternity jeans and a royal blue blouse that was nice and roomy. In the backseat there were half a dozen bags of other clothes she would need to finish out her pregnancy.

"Are you hungry?" he asked as he pulled into a parking space near the café.

"Starving," she replied. "What about you?"

"I'm hungry." He cut the engine and then got out of the truck and went around to the passenger door where she had gotten out, as well.

He immediately pulled her against his side and threw his arm around her shoulder. "You don't have to do that anymore," she said.

"Do what?"

"Hold me so close to protect me."

He grinned at her. "Darlin', I'm holding you close because I want to, because I love you."

She snuggled against him. "I like that about you."

They entered the busy café. Just like last time, an abrupt silence fell over the other diners. Flint's heart sank and Madison's chin shot up defensively.

And then somebody clapped. And that clap was followed by another…and another. As the two of them moved toward an empty booth, men got to their feet and women shouted words of encouragement and support.

Flint's heart swelled. This was the Bitterroot he knew, a place filled with good people who supported each other and formed a bond of community that couldn't be broken.

Happy tears raced down Madison's face. When

they sat down, the clapping finally stopped. She took her napkin and wiped away her tears. "Wow, I didn't expect that."

"You deserve it," Flint replied. "You took a monster off the streets all by yourself."

Waitress Jayme Lathrop greeted them with a bright smile and then her smile faltered. "Madison, I just want to thank you for what you did." Her brown eyes gazed at Madison intently.

"Were you the one who left a note for me?" Madison asked softly.

Jayme nodded. Madison immediately got up and pulled the young woman into her embrace. Flint had never loved Madison more as he watched her comfort a fellow victim of Brad's.

She whispered into Jayme's ear and then the two released each other and Madison scooted back into the seat. "Now, what can I get you two this evening?" Jayme smiled at them once again.

"What did you say to her?" Flint asked curiously when Jayme had left their booth.

"I told her if she ever needed to talk to somebody, I'm here for her. I also reminded her that she is a beautiful and strong woman, a survivor who has the right to hold her head up high."

"Do you have any idea how much I love you?" he asked.

"If it's half as much as I love you, then it's enough

for me," she replied. Her beautiful eyes sparkled with warmth and love.

This woman had given him an optimistic view of his life going forward. She intended to talk to the doctor to learn everything she could about his condition, a condition he now knew he could manage. He intended to talk to Cassie about quitting the ranch in the next week or so.

Eventually, he'd figure out what job he wanted to work and he'd continue to support his family. Madison had brought sunshine into what had become a dark place in his soul.

"I love you so much and even though I don't have a ring or anything right now, I want to propose to you," he said.

"So is that an official marriage proposal?" she asked teasingly.

"It is. I want to marry you, Madison. I want to marry you as soon as I can and have you by my side forever. I love you with all my heart."

She gazed at him for a long moment and in that space of time Flint's heart dipped. Had she changed her mind about him? Did she not want to marry him?

"Really?" she finally said. "You're going to propose to me in the middle of a noisy café without getting down on one knee and making it a little more official?"

Flint immediately slid out of the booth and dropped to one knee. "Madison Taylor…will you marry me?"

"Yes," she replied. She also got out of the booth and took his hands in hers. "Yes, yes, Flint. I'll marry you."

He got up and grabbed her into his arms and as he kissed her people hooted and hollered their approval. When the kiss ended she gazed up at him, her face glowing with happiness. "You're my forever cowboy, Flint, and I'll love you through eternity."

He kissed her once again, his heart filled with joy. This woman was his future, and the baby she carried was his in love. His cabin in the woods was now truly an enchanted place where love would live forever.

* * * * *

Don't forget previous titles in the
Cowboys of Holiday Ranch series:

Cowboy Defender
Guardian Cowboy
Sheltered by the Cowboy
Killer Cowboy
Operation Cowboy Daddy
Cowboy at Arms

Available now from
Harlequin Romantic Suspense!

She looked up at him, her expression stricken. "You don't
believe me either, do you? You don't think I can prove
that Russell was on to something real."

"I'm reserving judgment," he said, keeping his words
as steady as he could, "until I see more evidence. And
you might want to consider holding back on any more
accusations until you've recovered from this shock—and
you have that proof in hand."

"Oh, I'll find the proof. I have a good idea where, too.
All I have to do is get back to the turbines as soon as
possible and find the—"

"No way," he said sharply. "You're not going out
there. You saw the email, right? About Green Horizons'
safety review?"

She gave me a disgusted look. "Of course they want to
keep everyone away. If they're somehow involved in all

this, they'll drag out their review forever. And leave any evidence cleaned and sanitized for their own protection."

"Or they're trying to keep from being on the hook for any further accidents. Either way, I said no, Emma. I don't want you or your students taking any unnecessary chances."

"I'd never involve them. Never. After Russell, there's no way I would chance that." She shook her head, tears filling her eyes. "I was—I was the one to call Russell's parents. I insisted on it. It nearly killed me, breaking that news to them."

"Then you'll understand how I feel," Beau said, "when I tell you I'm not making that call to your folks, your boss or anyone else when you go getting yourself hurt again. Or worse."

She made a scoffing sound. "You've helped me out a couple times, sure. That doesn't make me your responsibility."

"That's where you're wrong, Dr. Copley. I take everyone who lives on, works on or sets foot on my spread as my responsibility," he said, sincerity ringing in his every word, "which is why, from this point forward, I'm barring you from Kingston property."

Don't miss
Deadly Texas Summer
by Colleen Thompson

Available March 2020 wherever
Harlequin Romantic Suspense
books and ebooks are sold.

Harlequin.com

Get 4 FREE REWARDS!

We'll send you 2 FREE Books plus 2 FREE Mystery Gifts.

Harlequin Romantic Suspense books are heart-racing page-turners with unexpected plot twists and irresistible chemistry that will keep you guessing to the very end.

FREE Value Over $20